"You've been pregn  gone?" Anger sharpens h me?"

A brittle laugh escape preoccupied."

"It's been six months, Liv. You've had plenty of time to tell me before now."

He was right, of course, but I was so angry at his accusations I couldn't admit it.

"Like you could have told me about Melanie? Or my parents could have told me about Junie? I don't think any of you needs to lecture me on being honest and forthright."

"So this was your payback? You were going to have my baby and raise it without me? And if you were lucky, I'd never find out? Is that what you thought?"

"Not really, no. To be honest, I wasn't sure you'd care."

Silence reigns for interminable seconds before he gives a shuddering sigh and runs his hand over my hair.

"Ah, Livy," he says sadly. "It really is over, isn't it?"

Other Books by Gloria Davidson Marlow

Silenced Songs
Broken Ties
When Swallows Fall
Sweet Sacrifices
Shades of Silence
The Butterfly Game
Flowers for Megan

Losing Us

by

Gloria Davidson Marlow

Losing Us

Cover Art by *Jennifer Greeff*

The Wild Rose Press, Inc.
PO Box 708
Adams Basin, NY 14410-0708
Visit us at www.thewildrosepress.com

Publishing History
First Edition, 2022
Trade Paperback ISBN 978-1-5092-4453-9
Digital ISBN 978-1-5092-4454-6

Published in the United States of America

Chapter One

Olivia

"Every great mistake has a halfway moment, a split second when it can be recalled and perhaps remedied."

As I stare into the passion-dazed eyes of my husband, I wonder if Pearl Buck was right when she wrote those words. Was there a moment when this mistake could have been recalled and remedied? If I had taken the time to dig my phone out of my purse on my way to his office, warning him that I was on my way, would he have taken the time to slip Melanie Evans' pert little breast back into her black lace bra? Would he have zipped his pants and brushed his hair into its normal lines? Would he have at least locked the door that joined his office with the reception area, or asked his secretary to stand watch outside? Was it my mistake to remedy, or was it his?

Our eyes meet over her perfectly formed, artificially tanned shoulder, and I know it's too late. If there ever was a halfway point, it is long since gone, and I wonder futilely when it passed us by and why we didn't notice.

The news I've come to tell him dies on my lips, and a cry of anguish that longs to be loosed takes its place. Without a sound, I turn and walk out the door, past his open-mouthed secretary, to the bank of elevators at the end of the hall.

"Olivia!" he cries behind me. I pick up my pace. "Livy, please wait!"

I jam the elevator button, then jam it again. I need to be in the safety of my own car before the sobs building in my chest break through. I need desperately to not be *that* wife, the one lying in a sobbing puddle at her husband's feet as he tries to explain why it's not what it appears to be.

"Olivia." He is just behind, so I push the button again and again, and for good measure, again. Anything but turn and look at him. His hand encircles my arm, and he pulls me around to face him. It's a gentle tug, but it does the trick, and I am face to face with him much sooner than I would have liked. "Please just listen to me."

His usually tan skin has lost some of its color, his dark eyes shimmer with tears, and he looks hopelessly lost.

Of its own accord, my hand reaches out and smooths his hair. It's an action as familiar to me as breathing, something I've done a million times before, but in that moment, I hate myself almost as much as I hate him.

A wave of sadness rolls through me. What happened to the people we once were? Where is the magical connection I always thought we had, the one that makes us better together than we are alone? A sob catches in my throat, and I purse my lips to silence it.

"I'm so sorry," Daniel says, his hands cupping my face and his thumbs gently wiping away my tears. This, too, is a familiar gesture, bringing back memories of those horrible nights and days that nearly destroyed us. "What happened to us, Liv?"

Could either of us really not know what happened?

Could we possibly be so dense? Or have we just become experts at lying to ourselves and each other? Had we been destroyed and not even realized it? Had he known all along? Was I the only one clinging to the illusion that we had survived?

We can pretend, of course, pretend that we don't remember those days, those hours, those moments. But every single second of what happened to us is there in that hallway, making the air thick enough to choke us both with pain and regret. As we've done for the last ten years, we silently ignore the pain, pushing it away with a desperation born of despair.

"I'm sorry," he murmurs again.

I know beyond a shadow of a doubt his words are true. He is sorry. Whether he was sorry an hour ago or only moments ago, when I found out, I don't know. Maybe I will care tomorrow or the next day or a year from now, but standing there, I don't care about his apologies, his reasons, or his questions.

Still, there is one thing I need to know. A question I don't even realize is coming, until it escapes my lips. I don't know if it's a question for the past, the present, or the future, only that it is there, right now, between us.

"Do you love her?"

"No." The answer is quick. He doesn't even give it any thought, and I see the truth of it in the shame on his face. "And she doesn't love me. We just enjoy each other."

"Aah," I say and nod my head as if I understand. What else can I say or do?

"You're the only woman I'll ever love, Liv," he says, his voice cracking. "My best friend."

"I won't be there when you get home."

"I know."

Behind me, the elevator doors slide open, and I turn my back to him. He puts out his hand to stop them from closing.

"Liv? Why did you come by? Was there something you needed?" he swallows hard. "I wasn't expecting you."

It is a cruel thing I do then. After all we've sacrificed to get pregnant, all the months of waiting, all the tears and worries, he deserves to know that I am. But I can't find it in me to tell him, so I shake my head.

"It was nothing," I say and step into the empty elevator.

Chapter Two

By the time I reach the car, I'm in a state of shock, gradually going numb as if I'm freezing from the inside out. I slide behind the wheel, buckle my seat belt, and pull out of the parking lot without conscious thought.

The temperature outside is ninety-five degrees, but I don't turn on the air conditioner. Ice has replaced the blood in my veins, and I am suffocating on the arctic film of it in my lungs. I roll the windows down, gasping at the hot, dry air that fills the car. I'm halfway to my parents' house before I realize my destination.

My phone begins to ring as I'm crossing the river. Daniel's office number flashes on the screen. I let it ring, and when it finally quits, I pull to the side of the road and get out. I hurl the phone as far as I can, smiling to myself when I hear the satisfying plunk of it hitting the water.

I park in my parents' driveway and sit in my car for a while, surveying the house where I grew up. It hasn't changed at all in the last two decades. As a teenager and young adult, I found it stagnant and stifling. Now, it's comforting to know that beyond the glass-paned front door, all is familiar and unchanging. From the shag carpet in the living room to the apple clock on the kitchen wall, nothing will have changed at all.

I see the living room curtain move, and I know my father, alerted to my arrival by his elderly Cairn terrier, Dooley, is peering out to see who has arrived. I take a deep breath and push myself out of the car.

The front door opens, and my dad is there, his kind gray eyes studying me as I come toward him. I stop just short of him, and a frown creases his brow. He doesn't ask questions or wait for a greeting. He simply offers me a sad smile and opens his arms.

I step into his embrace, and he hugs me tightly as I cry, and Dooley snuffles worriedly at our legs.

I hear the soft click of my mother's shoes on the wood floor before I hear her voice.

"Oliver? Did you say Olivia is here?" she calls down the hall, and then she is there, just behind him.

I can't see her because my face is still buried against my father's chest, but I can feel her presence. My mother is five feet and one inch tall compared to my father's six foot two and my own five foot five, but she has a presence that seems to fill up a room and take the air right out of it.

"Olivia?" her voice is panicked as she tries to see me around my father. "What on earth has happened? Did the doctor give you a bad report?"

Although I don't know how it's possible, I cry even harder.

"Come inside," she orders and pulls my father in by the sleeve. Wrapped in his arms, I have no choice but to follow. "Constance is probably already on the phone with half the neighborhood."

Constance Miller is the octogenarian who lives across the street. For as long as I can remember, she has been the neighborhood gossipmonger, the source of every rumor and every truth circulated in our neighborhood. I wish wildly that she had been privy to Daniel's affair, perhaps then my life wouldn't have come crashing down about me without warning.

Once we're inside, Mama quickly maneuvers around us until she can get hold of my arm and pull me away from Daddy and into the living room. She nudges me onto the sofa, and I sit, perched on the edge, my hands clenched around the wad of tissues she has forced into them.

"What is it, Olivia?" she demands, her stern voice laced with worry. "Is it Daniel?"

I know my mother well enough to know she has reached the conclusion that my husband is dead. This is the worst-case scenario, and my mother will always go to the worst-case scenario before anything else. Still, I nod without explanation. Let her think he's dead. For just a moment, I entertain the thought that this would be better than the truth, but I know that isn't true. Death has touched us, Daniel and me, and it is infinitely worse than anything else imaginable.

"Is he hurt? Dead?"

I shake my head.

"For goodness' sake, Olivia!" she scolds. "Tell us what's happened. What has he done?"

"Melanie Evans," her name snaps out, as if my mother even has a clue who she is, or that it answers her question. I think of Melanie, back and shoulders exposed, one of Daniel's hands splayed across her bare skin, the other cupping her small firm breast, and my breath catches in my throat. I can barely push the words past my lips. "He's having an affair with Melanie Evans."

"Aha."

Surprised by the nonchalant response, I lift my gaze to hers. She frowns and gives me a kind of half shrug before turning to look at my father. "Oliver, go fix us some tea."

He rises obediently and disappears down the hall.

I prepare myself for questions about my husband's lover, about how I learned about the affair, about what was said, how I feel, what I plan to do.

Instead, Mama looks me in the eye, her sympathy replaced by something hard and stern. And without one single question, she says, "You'll forgive him, of course."

I must stare at her as if she has lost her mind, because she grimaces and waves her hand in dismissal.

"Men are weak, Olivia. It's a woman's duty to forgive them their weaknesses and go about her business."

I can't decide whether I want to slam my hands over my ears or her mouth. How can she even begin to spout such archaic platitudes to me? I gather my icy anger around me like a cloak and meet her eyes.

"What business do we go about, Mother?" I ask, as if I care. I work mornings in the Exhibitions Department at the Brailing Art Museum downtown, and three afternoons a week, I teach classes for the children's program at the museum. Although I love my work at the museum, nothing I do there is my life. My life for the last ten years has been Daniel. And making a baby. Maybe not in that order.

"Whatever your business was yesterday—or this morning, or two seconds before you found out—continues to be your business." She peers over her glasses at me. "We take a deep breath, pull ourselves together, and pick up wherever we left off. We carry on."

"I don't want to carry on," I say. "Not with him."

I'm not sure if this is true, of course. It's too early. Maybe we can move past it, but I sincerely doubt it. Still, there is the baby to consider, so I'm not certain I really have a choice. I can almost hear my inner modern woman roar at the thought. *Of course, I have a choice*, she cries, *I don't need a man to raise a baby.*

"I know you don't," my mother says confusing me for a minute. Is she agreeing with my not wanting to be with him, or my ability to raise a baby alone? "It's impossible for you to imagine forgiving him right now, but you might change your mind. Just don't do anything permanent yet."

I nod. Of course, I won't call a divorce attorney today. I need time to think, time for my brain to thaw and my thoughts to start processing again.

"Tea's on the table," Daddy says, coming back into the room. "I made us some sandwiches, too."

When I push to my feet, I'm suddenly unbalanced, and the room grows a bit dim around me. I hear Mama's gasp and feel Daddy's hands around my arms, pushing me back to the sofa. I lean my head against my knees until I feel steady again.

"It's just your nerves," Mama assures me, but I shake my head against my knees as I begin to cry again.

I lift my face to hers. "It's not just nerves. I'm pregnant."

Her face lights up for a moment before her own eyes fill with tears. She stands and walks toward the kitchen, leaving my father to help me up and follow in her wake.

****

"You need to talk to Junetta," my mother says into the silence that has reigned in the kitchen for the last fifteen minutes.

9

I have picked at my sandwich, attempted to choke down a few bites, and gulped iced tea like a man dying of thirst. My eyes have watched the hands of the familiar apple-shaped clock on the far wall, as I try to guess how long it has been now since my world collapsed. I'm not used to my mother not trying to fix things as soon as they go wrong, so the silence has been especially deafening when such a monumental thing has gone wrong here.

Of all the things I imagine my mother saying, this is not one of them. I can think of no reason at all that she would bring up Aunt Junie, my father's sister, at this exact moment.

"Why?"

"Sylvia." Is it a plea or a warning I hear in the quiet way my father says her name?

They exchange a look, and I feel my stomach clench in dread. For just a moment, I am back in Daniel's office, facing him over Melanie's shoulder, wishing I hadn't come. Wishing we could have stopped this mistake. I recognize this look between my parents. I've seen it before over the years, and as it always has, it scares the hell out of me.

He runs a hand through his shock of white hair, making it stand on end. It's always been a bit unruly, especially compared to Mama's neatly curled brown bob, but tonight, it stands straight on end.

With a sigh, my father surrenders the silent battle between them, and places his hand on mine.

"Honey, you know your mother and I weren't young when you were born, and there weren't any more children after you."

I open my mouth to tell him to be quiet. I don't want him to make this mistake.

By today's standards, my parents weren't all that old when I was born. My mother was thirty-nine and my father forty-two. By the standards of the times, however, they were ancient. The fact that there weren't any more children hadn't escaped me either, of course. I clearly remember hounding Mama when I was a child, begging in vain for a brother or sister.

"The truth is, Olivia, your mother and I weren't able to have any children. We tried for years. Finally, we realized it just wasn't in the cards for us."

For a moment, I don't comprehend what he's saying, but I know this is the halfway moment, the moment when we can still avert this mistake.

"You mean you couldn't have any *other* children?" My heart begs for him to recall it, remedy it, not to make what he's about to say real.

"No, Olivia, we couldn't have *any* children."

Just like that, the split second is gone, and we have crossed the halfway moment. I can't go back, and I can't go forward. I think wildly that this is how someone stuck on a train track must feel as the train barrels toward them, lights flashing, horn blaring. Like them, I can only sit there in my mother's kitchen and absorb the impact into my very soul.

"I'm not yours?" I whisper.

Mama speaks then.

"You're ours, Olivia. You're more ours than you are anyone else's. Don't you forget that. You will always be ours." She starts crying, and Daddy smooths his hand over her back.

"We adopted you," he says as if I need that clarification.

"Well, I guess I should be glad you didn't kidnap

me," I say, anger and fear making me sound far more flippant than I feel. "Although wanting to avoid prison would at least explain why you never told me I wasn't yours to begin with."

"Olivia!" Mama gasps. "How can you be so cruel?"

"Cruel?" I cry. "How can you consider me cruel when you've had this secret for thirty-five years? Thirty-five years, Mama! And you never thought to tell me before now?"

"Of course we thought about telling you," Daddy says, but I am beyond listening to anything that sounds even remotely positive from either of them.

"Why now? Were you waiting for just such a day? The day my marriage ended?" My voice rises to a pitch I don't even recognize as my own, and I can feel my entire body beginning to shake. "What a perfect day to let me in on the huge family secret!" I force myself to take deep calming breaths. I look at my mother and calmly repeat my earlier question. "Why should I talk to Aunt Junie?"

She looks like a deer in the headlights. As if she suddenly realizes there's no going back. As if she too realizes we've passed the halfway point and there's no choice but to stand there and wait for the end.

"Junetta is your mother," Daddy whispers. "She couldn't keep you. So she gave you to us."

Mama is crying, and Daddy looks close to it as they wait to see my reaction. The truth is, I don't know how to react. I have no idea what a woman does when her entire life becomes a lie in one day.

I stand up.

Mama is beside me in an instant. I say nothing as she follows me up the stairs, her hand out as if I may fall over at any moment. I've been pregnant once before, and this is the way she acted the entire nine months. Was she ever tempted to tell me the truth then?

When we get to my room, she pulls back my covers and tucks me in as if I'm still a child. Before she leaves, she kisses my forehead, and I once again breathe in the scent of Timeless perfume. This time, the familiarity of it hurts.

"We love you, Olivia," she whispers.

I want to deny her the words, but I can't make myself do it.

"I know, Mama. I love you, too."

I lie in the dark of my former bedroom, my heart pounding and my head spinning with questions and thoughts I can't control. I pray fervently for peace or whatever it will take for me to continue to breathe and function until this nightmare is over. The ice that seemed to encase me on the way from Daniel's office is back, freezing me from the inside out. I lie there, shivering, teeth chattering so hard I think my parents must surely hear it wherever they are. Finally, the chills subside, and I doze off.

What seems like hours later, Dooley's sharp yap wakes me up. I hear my father's low voice shushing him, followed by the sound of the back door closing and the click of the lock. I listen to the sound of my parents coming up the stairs, and my mother stopping in my doorway. I hold my breath, releasing it only when she moves away. I can't talk or feel or cry any more, not tonight. Maybe not ever again.

When I'm sure my parents are in bed, I get up and shuffle to the bathroom. I study my reflection in the mirror. Is it only my imagination that makes me think I look different than I did this morning? That woman had known who she was, or she had at least had a firm grasp on the illusion. Daniel Carson's wife, Oliver and Sylvia Darlington's daughter. I squeeze my eyes shut, trying to blot out the waves of pain and betrayal that threaten to swallow me whole. I am no longer that woman. In many ways, I suppose I never was. I take a few deep steadying breaths and open my eyes.

I meet my own gaze, so familiar and yet so changed, and I realize I feel nothing. At last, I am completely numb.

Chapter Three

Two days later, I'm on a plane to Miami.

Junetta Darlington is my father's younger sister, and an actress who starred in movies and television shows in the seventies and eighties. Even years later, people often recognized her on the street, and I remember how proud I was when they would point out the resemblance between us or when one of my friends realized who she was. Mama, however, assured me that acting in B movies and being a guest star on television did not make one a movie star. She worked hard to quell any hopes I may have had about following in Junie's footsteps.

After she quit acting and moved to Key West, Aunt Junie seemed to have given her eccentricity her full attention, as if she meant to live a life that left people like my mother sputtering in dismay.

After each visit to or from Aunt Junie, Mama would make the same pronouncement, without fail.

"Oliver," she'd say to my father as she shook her head in what I can only describe as amazement, "that Junie is as crazy as a bed bug."

"Always has been," he'd say without even looking up from the evening paper.

When I was eight, I told Aunt Junie that Mama thought she was crazy.

With a chuckle, Aunt Junie shrugged.

"There's all kinds of crazy, Livy, darling," she said,

and I nodded as if I understood what she meant. "You just have to hope you're lucky enough to get to choose your own crazy."

As the plane starts its descent, I remember those words, and for the first time, they make perfect sense. I wonder if the craziest of all aren't those of us living what seem on the outside like perfectly normal lives.

Aunt Junie lives in a conch house on a large lot in Key West. A saltwater pool separates the main house from three cottages set in a semicircle behind it. The residents of those cottages were the reasons I was never allowed to visit Aunt Junie unless one of my parents was with me.

Corliss and Dianna lived in one of the small houses together. The first time I heard Mama say they were lesbians, I was six. I had no idea what in the world that meant, but it was spoken in such hushed tones, with such horror, that I could only surmise it was some dreadful and contagious disease, like the leprosy I'd learned about in Sunday School. All these years later, I'm not sure Mama was right about them, but there is no changing her mind once she decides something is true.

In the second house was Opal Horowitz, a tiny woman with a towering platinum beehive, who made extra money performing séances and reading people's fortunes. To my mother, she was the devil incarnate, and I was ordered never to look at her or even acknowledge she existed. My usually practical mother was terrified of a hex being put on us.

The final house was occupied by Harry Tyndale. Harry was a slim, bespectacled man with sharp features, a curled mustache, and a pointed beard. He was the author of a series of beautifully illustrated nature books for children. My mother always called him Aunt Junie's paramour, and from her disgust, I could only surmise as a child that his chosen profession, like Opal's, was one only the lowest form of sinner would choose. Still, I had a copy of every one of his books on my bookshelf as a child.

As children, we are given no background information about the characters inhabiting our lives. Our parents form their own ideas and feed those ideas to us as the truth, leaving us no choice but to accept them as such.

My mother's ideas about people were often formed by her own assumptions and judgments, which were a bone of contention between us more than once. It is only now, when I compare my own differences with my mother to her differences with Junie that I see the connection between the two.

I smooth my hand over my belly. My own child grows there, and I vow to be honest and forthright with him or her. Guilt rears its ugly head as I think of Daniel. How can I possibly judge anyone's honesty or dishonesty when I'm keeping such a secret from him? I know if I tell him about the baby, he'll want to reconcile. I also know that it might be the best thing to do. But I can't make myself do it. I can't quit thinking about the look in his eyes when I came into his office, nor can I stop the envy that shoots through me every time I think of it. I wish I could tell myself I'm jealous of Melanie, but the fact is I'm not only jealous my husband was with another woman. I'm jealous that they enjoyed each other. I'm jealous of the passion I saw in his eyes. I envy what he found in her arms.

I can't forget the jolt of recognition I felt when our

17

eyes met, before reality set in, and he realized I was there in his office, his mistress between us. When was the last time he looked like that when we made love? I control a bitter chuckle as I wonder when the last time we actually made love *was*. Sex as often as possible, when the time is right and all the stars align, but it is only a means to an end. Something we have to do to get pregnant.

I lean my head back against the seat and close my eyes, trying to remember what it felt like to be lost in passion. I give up when the plane touches down on the runway.

Miami International Airport is a hectic place, but Aunt Junie is easy to spot. Dressed in a red-and-gold caftan, and a small gold turban, she lifts her arm to wave at me. Ruby-studded bangles catch the sun, flashing like a beacon in the light.

I tug my cardigan closed over my fitted red sheath dress. My mother, Sylvia, hates the color red. Aunt Junie loves it. I am in tune enough with myself to know that I picked this particular dress because of its color, but I'm not sure if I wore it to injure the one woman or please the other.

I have a long history of flaunting Aunt Junie in Mama's face. What teenager doesn't find those buttons to push and use them to her advantage? Aunt Junie is and has always been Mama's button. I have no doubt that some of my fascination with Aunt Junie was because of Mama's disapproval of her. I know now that at least some of Mama's disapproval was because of my fascination with the woman who had given birth to me.

Had my heart somehow known what my head did not? Had that been where the connection I felt to her came from? I always thought my fascination was simply because she was so different than anyone else I knew, with her flowing dresses, bejeweled sandals, and nonchalance in the face of Mama's censure. The older I got, the more I had admired that nonchalance and the more I had wanted to emulate it.

When I was sixteen, I skipped school and rode the bus down to Key West. It was a long ride, cutting through the middle of the state and back to the coast, but I was knocking on her door before sunset.

I remember that day like it was yesterday. I knocked and was granted entry by Aunt Junie's rich voice echoing across the Italian tiled floors of the house. A thick, potent smell I recognized immediately greeted me as I came down the hall and into what was once the parlor, a room I had never been allowed in before.

I stopped and stared in awe at the smoke-shrouded tableau before me. Like a scene out of a movie, the parlor was reminiscent of a sultan's bedchamber. Silk and velvet fabric in dark, rich hues hung from the ceiling and covered the walls. Large swathes of the same rich fabric were spread about on the furniture and floor, interspersed with luxurious blankets of various furs. The centerpiece of the room was an immense plush sofa, upholstered in red-and-gold velvet brocade, and replete with dozens of pillows. It was accompanied by a matching divan, a few low mahogany tables, and a half dozen large floor pillows and velvet-covered poofs. The room was decorated with paintings and various oddities that Harry and Aunt Junie collected in their travels around the world.

Aunt Junie lay on the sofa, her head in Harry's lap and her feet hanging over one end. Corliss and Diana lounged on the pillows scattered over the floor, and

Opal's tiny body was nearly swallowed in the billowing depths of the divan. I wondered giddily if the hose running from the hookah on the table to her brightly painted lips was a lifeline keeping her from disappearing completely.

I knew then why Aunt Junie usually kept the door to this room closed.

"That's my magical, mystical harem room," she had laughed when I asked her once what was behind the door. I was six, and my curiosity was instantly piqued.

"Junetta, for heaven's sake, don't tell her that!" Mama exclaimed as she clamped her hands over my ears.

"Oh, Sylvie, don't be such a stick-in-the-mud. You know, if you came down from your high horse and joined us once in a while, you might loosen up a bit. You might even enjoy it."

Aunt Junie's eyes sparkled with merriment as Mama brushed past her and hurried me to the car.

So when I showed up there, suitcase in hand, no Sylvia and Oliver in tow, I thought she would laugh it off and let me hide out there a day or two. Instead, she rose from her place on the sofa and walked toward me, her waist-length black hair swaying against her hips. When she reached me, she took my arm and led me away from the room, closing the door behind her.

"Get your ass in that kitchen and call your mother," she commanded.

"But Aunt Junie, she's—"

She raised a hand to stop me. "I don't care why you're here, Olivia. You can stay tonight, but you're going home first thing in the morning. And you are calling Sylvia and Oliver right now."

Once I told my parents where I was, she took the

phone from me and assured them she would put me on a bus home the next morning.

"I know Sylvia's no walk in the park, sweetheart," she said after she'd hung up the phone. "But don't ever use me to hurt her again."

Then, like the Aunt Junie I'd always known, she kissed my cheek, poured me a glass of soda, and told me to make myself at home.

As we reach each other now, Aunt Junie hugs me tightly before holding me out at arm's length so she can see my face.

"Sylvia told me what he did," she says, her voice a mixture of anger and pity.

I say nothing, and she nods her head as if coming to a decision.

"We'll talk about it all later. For now, you'll just rest and relax." She smiles, albeit a bit sadly. "You have to take care of yourself and the baby."

She places her hand through my arm and leads me toward the luggage carousels. As we go, I catch a glimpse of us in a window. Our differences are clear, with me in my conservative dress and her in her long, flowing robe. Yet, for the first time, I also see the similarities. I wonder if Mama and Aunt Junie have always seen them. I can't help but wonder which of them it bothered more.

Chapter Four

Daniel

In the decade we've been married, I can only recall a handful of times I've come home to an empty house. Even then, I've always known where Olivia was and had an idea of when she'd be home. Now, although I know she's at her parents' house, I have no idea if she'll ever be home again.

I sink onto the couch and cover my face with my hands. I want to call her, to beg her to forgive me and come home, but it all sounds like such a crock. For God's sake, she walked in on me with another woman's tit in my hand.

What was I thinking? I ask myself this question for the millionth time, even though I know the truth. I wasn't thinking. Not the first time I had sex with Melanie and not the last. There was enough thinking going on when Olivia and I had sex. With Melanie, it hadn't required any thought at all.

I know there are no excuses for what I've done. Even so, there are reasons.

Olivia is the only woman I have ever loved. I have never doubted or second-guessed my love for her or her love for me. But she's changed so much in the last few years I barely recognize her anymore. Truthfully, I find it less painful to be with a virtual stranger like Melanie than a stranger I once knew. A stranger I still love.

There was a time when Olivia was a common sight at my office. She came by on her lunch break, her afternoons off from the museum, or whenever else she could find time. She'd tell my secretary she was there to kidnap me before she came into my office and proceeded to do just that. We usually didn't make it very far. The elevator, the empty office down the hall, the large storage closet on the fourth floor, even the car. We made love anywhere we could, and we enjoyed every minute of it and our life together. It may sound corny, but we weren't just lovers, we were best friends.

Olivia is the most beautiful woman I've ever seen. With a mane of dark curls, eyes as blue as the sky, and a perfectly voluptuous figure, she caught my attention the very first time I laid eyes on her waiting tables at Carlton's on Main. The quickness of her smile and the warmth of her laughter drew me like a moth to a flame. I could think of nothing else until I finally worked up the nerve to talk to her.

Despite her easy laughter and friendliness, she was quiet and shy, preferring to hide out in the school library at night rather than hang out with her friends. Though my friends didn't understand it, I suddenly found I liked the art history section of the library better than anywhere else in town.

From the first time I saw her, I never looked at anyone else, never wanted anyone else. All I wanted was to love and be loved by Olivia Darlington.

I asked her to marry me on Christmas Eve our senior year in college, and the following autumn we were married in the church where she grew up.

By then, I was working as an architect at Jasper and

James, and she was teaching art history to eighth graders.

We were married three years when she got pregnant, and I'm not ashamed to say it was the most miraculous thing I've ever witnessed. I watched as she grew rounder and more beautiful with each passing day. I watched as our child moved inside of her, felt his energetic movements against my hand.

I was there when they placed our tiny son in Olivia's arms, and I was there when they took him away for the last time. I was there when Olivia collapsed against his miniature coffin, crying as if her heart would never heal. Though I longed to do the same, I knew that only one of us could give in to it, and I felt certain it was something a mother deserved to be able to do.

He had been gone for four years when Olivia decided she wanted to get pregnant again. She stopped using birth control, and we waited for it to happen.

Six years later we were still waiting, but Olivia's patience was gone. In the last year, we'd started what seemed an endless round of doctors who told us what we should do. Still, no matter how well we followed their directions, it didn't happen.

Making love was over for us. Instead, we had sex that was as perfunctory as taking out the garbage or filling the bird feeder out back. It became just one more thing staring me in the face like one of the chores on the "honey-do" list we kept on the refrigerator.

Fix the step, mow the grass, make me pregnant. Only, while I could do all the rest on my own schedule, she must be made pregnant on her body's schedule, so she watched the clock and the calendar like a hawk. She no longer came to the office or spontaneously grabbed me and pulled me down to the couch or the kitchen floor.

I could no longer elicit a response with a touch or a look, and God forbid I tried to coax her down to the floor or the couch or anywhere there weren't three pillows to lift her ass while we had sex. Instead, everything must be timed and ready for that exact moment when pregnancy was practically guaranteed to happen.

Guarantee or no, however, month after month passed without a hint of a baby. And with each passing day, my beautiful, sweet, spontaneous wife became an unhappy, nagging bitch who could barely stand the sight of me.

I know that sounds harsh, and there are times when I catch a glimpse of the woman I married. But those glimpses have become fewer and farther between with each childless day. Truth is I can hardly miss her now, when only her body has been with me for years. I can only assume she feels the same way about me. I've not been an exact walk in the park myself.

I stand up and move to the window. Staring sightlessly into the darkness outside, I wonder whether I should call her or not.

Even though she didn't react with the fury I expected, I know Olivia is angry and hurt. As soon as I looked up and saw her there in the doorway, I knew it hadn't been worth it. Nothing could ever be worth the emptiness that seemed to engulf my pretty blue-eyed bride as she stared at me over another woman's shoulder.

My heart aches as I think of her soft hand smoothing my hair while she waited for the elevator. I can't control the tears as I turn out the lights and lie down on the couch. Comfortable or not, there is no way I can face our empty bed tonight.

I wait three days before calling her at work. I've tried her cell phone a few times, but she isn't answering it. The woman who answers the phone tells me she's taken an extended leave of absence. She isn't anyone I recognize, and I realize that while Olivia knows many of my co-workers, I have never met most of hers. I know that her boss, who I have met a time or two, quit a few months ago and was replaced by someone Olivia isn't crazy about. For the life of me, I can't remember his name, and I wonder if Olivia ever actually told me what it was. I know her friend Amy left after she had a baby last year, and her friend Mindy is due any day. I don't know if she intends to continue working after her baby is born or not. I wonder if Olivia quit talking to me about her job or if I just quit listening to what she was saying.

My next call is to her parents, although I hate the thought of talking to either of them. Though I hope Oliver will answer, it is Sylvia who picks up. Her voice grows cold when she realizes it's me.

"She isn't here, Daniel," she snaps without offering any further information.

"Sylvia, I'm really sorry for what happened."

"Well, yes, I'm sure you are. But that doesn't really change the fact that it did happen. It doesn't really help anything, does it?"

"Is she okay?" The words come out quickly, panicky almost. There is nothing I can do to change what has happened, but I don't want to think I've destroyed us forever.

"Yes."

"Do you know when she'll be back?"

"No."

"Will you tell her I called?"

"When I talk to her." A brief pause. "I have no idea when that will be. She's gone away for a while."

"Gone away?" I repeat. "Where the hell is she gone away to?"

"There's really no need for you to curse at me," my mother-in-law scolds.

"That wasn't really cursing, Sylvia. Now, would you please tell me where my wife is?"

"No," she says and hangs up. I curse loud and long, wishing Sylvia was standing here to witness it. I can just imagine her disapproval. When I'm done, I pick up the phone again.

This time when she answers, Sylvia's voice already holds the familiar frosty tone she saves for people who annoy her.

"If you continue to harass us, I will call the police, Daniel. I promise."

Again, the distinct click of the phone fills my ears.

"Damn it," I growl as I grab my keys and wallet from the counter. I hate going to Sylvia's, but the woman has left me no choice. She may be able to shelter Olivia from my phone calls, but it will be a tad harder to dismiss me when I'm standing on her front porch.

"For heaven's sake, Daniel, I told you she wasn't here," Sylvia says when she opens her front door, a dishtowel clutched in her hand.

"You're lying, Sylvia. I know she's here. Where else would she be? Now, let me see her."

"Olivia isn't here, and even if she were, I wouldn't let you see her. You broke her heart!" With that, she bursts into tears and covers her face with the dishtowel.

I take a step toward her and put my hand on her shoulder. No matter that she drives me up the wall most of the time, she is Olivia's mother and has been my mother-in-law for years. I've come to love her in spite of myself, and I hate the fact that I've hurt her and Oliver, too. She quickly gets hold of herself and shakes my hand off.

"Go home, Daniel," she says. "Olivia's gone to visit Junetta. I don't know when she'll be back."

"Why is she at Junie's?"

"That's no longer your concern," she informs me. She slips back through the door, and I hear the lock click into place before I can stop her.

Chapter Five

I continue going to the office, hoping it will lessen
the loneliness of our empty house, but all it does is
heighten my awareness of just how stupid I am. A
million memories of Olivia follow me no matter where I
am. At home, I see her in every room, laughing, talking,
loving me like no one else ever has or ever will. On the
street, I see her everywhere. Even the peach-colored drift
roses that grow in the bank parking lot across the street
from my office bring her to mind. How many times did
she comment on their beauty, or lay one on my desk
when she came by?

I lock myself in my office every day, and every day
as the bolt hits home, some small part of me wonders
why I wasn't so conscientious the day Olivia caught me
with Melanie. I think of that moment when she burst
through the door, and I curse myself for every type of
fool. I see her there over and over, the excitement on her
face, replaced by shock, then pain. While I wait for the
elevator, I see her as she stepped into the elevator, never
looking back at me as the doors closed and she was gone.

For two weeks, I avoid Melanie and she avoids me.
Then, as I'm packing up to leave on a Friday afternoon,
she slips into my office. She closes the door behind her
and comes toward me. She perches on the edge of my
desk, her short black skirt hiking up to show her bony
knees. The lowcut top she wears hangs loose about her

small breasts, exposing too much tanned skin. Gold earrings hang from her ears, which are uncovered by the close-cropped haircut she favors. Red lipstick graces her lips, and I can't help but think it is a garish color Olivia would never wear. Before the first day we slept together, I never looked twice at Melanie Evans. I can't imagine now what made me look at her then. It isn't that she's not a good-looking woman, but she isn't my type of woman.

A long red fingernail caresses my hand, and I raise my eyes to her. Lips pursed into a small smile, she stares at me knowingly.

"It's over, isn't it?" she asks. "With us, I mean."

"Yes," I answer, thinking I should try to sound more regretful than I do.

But Melanie is totally unemotional now, just as she always is. Her perfectly applied makeup never looks any different after making love than it does before, no matter how passionate the sex. No real emotion is involved. Perhaps that promise is what I first saw in her.

Olivia is all emotion. At the movies, at church, even curled up on the couch reading, she's prone to cry until her mascara turns her eyes black and she looks like a raccoon. Her lipstick never has stayed where it belonged when we made out, and there's nothing sexier than finding the print of her lips on the rim of her coffee cup or a tissue she's left lying on the bathroom counter.

Once upon a time, she made love to me with the same wild abandon with which she laughs and cries. It was enthusiastic, all-encompassing, and totally irresistible. Though I often thought of our lovemaking in recent years as unemotional, I realize now that there was still emotion involved. Fear, pain, sadness, and wary hope were between us every single time we came together, and suddenly I know it's emotion, not the lack thereof, that has driven us apart.

"It was fun, wasn't it?" Melanie says, bringing my attention back to her.

"That it was, Melanie." I won't lie and say I didn't enjoy having sex with her, but I can honestly say it was a purely physical affair. We didn't hang out together, eat meals together, have meaningful conversation, or anything else that would create a deeper relationship. We did what we did, and we went our separate ways.

"But it wasn't real." She slides off my desk and walks to the window. "Affairs are like that. They may look real. They may even feel real at times. But when it all comes down to it, they're just an illusion. A substitute for the real feeling, the real touch, the real person who will make our lives complete."

I am dumbfounded by the accuracy of her statement.

"You've already found that person," she says a bit wistfully. "Olivia's your real thing. I knew the first time I met you that you already had it. You didn't even spare me a second glance. That's not usually how it works, you know. But I realized you were firmly anchored in reality. Until a few months ago, I never thought I had a chance with you. Then one day we passed each other, and I saw it, that look I'd never seen from you before. I moved right in. I'd been waiting too long to let the chance pass me by. But I always knew it wasn't real between us. It never could be, because even if you were trying to escape it, you already had 'real' at home."

"Not anymore," I say miserably.

"She'll be back," she assures me with a friendly pat on my shoulder. She leaves my office without a backward glance.

****

The nights are endless without Olivia at home. I miss her soft warm body curled up next to me and the weird, kind of sexy, little noises she makes in her sleep.

Her book is still open on her nightstand, although she came and picked her reading glasses up. Her toothbrush and makeup are gone from the bathroom, and her side of the closet is noticeably emptier than it was before. I came home a day or two after she left, and it was obvious she had come while I was at work. I try to take comfort in the fact that she left some things. I tell myself that means she's planning on coming home. But with each day of silence between us, it's getting harder and harder to believe that.

She's been gone a month when I finally pick up the phone and call her at Junie's. For weeks, I've tried to convince myself I shouldn't call. I know I deserve it if she won't speak to me, but I still have to try. If nothing else, I just need to know she's okay.

Junie answers on the second ring, and I can feel her hostility. I half expect her to refuse to allow me to talk to Olivia, but she tells me to hang on, and in a moment, I hear her calling Olivia's name.

"If you don't want to talk to him, you just give me the word and I'll be happy to tell him so," Junie says loud enough for me to hear.

"Hello?" Olivia finally says into the phone. I breathe a sigh of relief.

"I'm so sorry, Olivia." I want to say something more, but there is nothing more to say.

"I know," she says, her voice a dull monotone that worries me with its lack of emotion.

"I tried to call your cell phone."

"It's at the bottom of the river."

I don't ask her how it got there or why.

"I thought you'd be at your parents' house. I went there looking for you."

"I'm not."

"Why are you at Junie's?"

She takes a deep breath, and for a minute, I think she's going to explain.

"I've got to go, Daniel."

"Please come home so we can talk," I plead. I need her here. I need to see her, to hold her, to convince her that I love her.

"I don't want to talk," she says. "Or come home."

"But you are coming home, right? To your parents' house anyway?"

"I don't know."

"But, Liv," I begin, before realizing I have no right to pressure her to come home when it was my mistake that drove her away. "I love you."

She hesitates a moment, and I know she is weighing the truth of my words, hopefully even trying to decide whether to repeat them herself. Finally, she takes another deep breath.

"Good-bye, Daniel," she says and hangs up.

Chapter Six

Olivia

I lie in bed with the windows open, listening to the quiet sounds of the night. On the wind, I can hear the faint strains of the music from Duval Street and smell the tinge of the ocean. The mixture stirs something within me, and in the blink of an eye, the Novocain-like effects of shock wear off and I am suddenly, achingly aware of every feeling I've been denying for the past two months.

I recall the jubilation I felt as Dr. Samuels confirmed my pregnancy. Though I had suspected it, I didn't tell Daniel. I didn't want to get his hopes up only to have to tell him I was wrong. How different things would be if I had told him. He would have gone to the doctor with me. I would never have caught him with Melanie. My parents would never have felt the need to unburden their secret. I could have gone on being lied to by everyone I love and never been the wiser.

Betrayal rips through me as I lie there in my borrowed bed, and I can no longer control my sorrow. I roll to my side and cry myself to sleep.

****

I am just stepping out of the shower the next morning when the phone rings. As I've done every time since the last time I talked to Daniel, I pray it isn't for me, but Dianna calls my name from downstairs. I groan as I reach for the phone beside my bed.

"Hello?"

"Olivia?" I expect my mother or Daniel, so I'm surprised to hear my best friend Julie's voice. "Are you okay? I've been telling Earl to ask you and Daniel over for weeks, and he's been putting me off. Then, finally last night, he tells me that you've left Daniel and are down in the Keys. I called your mother and got this number."

Did Earl have to tell her why I left, or had she already known? Was it possible Julie sat at my table just a few days before I left, eating shrimp scampi, sipping wine, and knowing my husband was screwing another woman?

"Did he tell you why I left?"

"Yes," she says, anger and sadness mingling in the silence that follows the admission.

"Did you know?"

"Of course not! How could you even think that?"

"I don't know," I say miserably. "I don't know what to think."

"Listen to me, Liv. If I'd thought for one minute that moron was cheating on you, I'd have beat the hell out of him when we were at your house for dinner."

The thought of petite, soft-spoken Julie beating the hell out of anyone makes me laugh in spite of myself.

"Did Earl know?"

"Oh, Liv, you know he did." She sighs. "That's why he's sleeping on the couch."

I begin to cry, then, and Julie gives a cluck of distress.

"Don't cry, sweetie. It'll all work out in the end."

"Have you seen him?"

"No, he doesn't dare come around here right now, and Earl says he avoids everyone at work. Earl called your house to check on him, but Daniel told him he just wanted to be left alone."

"Is Melanie with him?"

"No, not according to Earl." She pauses. "Why are you at Junie's anyway? I thought you'd be at your mom and dad's."

"I was at first, but then I thought I'd like to get farther away. You know how my mom is. She would have smothered me with concern. So I came down here where I could think."

"When are you coming home?"

"I don't know. I don't even know where to go if I come back. I can't very well kick Daniel out of the house." He inherited our house from the aunt who raised him after his parents died. I would never even think of living there without him, much less fighting him over it.

"You can come home and stay with us if you need to. Haley has a full bed. You can have her room. She can sleep in Cam's room or on the sofa in the playroom."

"Thanks for the offer, but I just need to be here right now." I want to tell her about the baby, but she's notoriously bad at keeping secrets—I should have known she didn't know about Daniel and Melanie. If she had known, I'd have known. She's going to be ecstatic about the baby and will be bursting with the news. She'll tell Earl as soon as we hang up, if she can keep quiet that long, and Daniel will know within minutes. I'm not ready for that. "I've got to run, but I'll call you in a few days."

I have no sooner hung up the phone than it begins to ring again. This time, I answer it, not at all surprised to hear my mother's voice on the other end.

"Did Julie call you? I hoped you wouldn't mind me giving her Junie's number."

"Yes, she called. I don't mind you giving her the number."

"I was hoping she would talk some sense into you. Tell you to come home."

"I'm not coming home right now." I tell her this every time she calls, which has gone from twice a day every day to every other day in the last week or so. I'm sure Dad told her to give me some space. I can't count how many times he's told her this in the past thirty-five years. It speaks to how worried she is that she's suddenly decided to take his advice.

"If you want to save your marriage, you need to come home, Olivia!"

I let out a sigh. So much for giving me space.

"I don't know if I want to save my marriage."

"Of course you want to save your marriage! You're having a baby. Daniel's baby. You have to come home and work things out."

"How are you and Dad doing, Mom? How's Dooley?"

"We're fine. The dog is fine. Why in heaven's name would you even ask about the dog? You have far more important things to worry about."

"I don't want to worry about those things today, though. So I'll worry about the dog."

"Don't be silly, Olivia."

"Listen, Mom, I was just on my way out the door. Going shopping for some maternity clothes."

Silence greets this announcement, and then in a small, tight voice, she asks, "Is Junie going with you?"

I can almost feel her pain. For a split second, I'm tempted to say yes, but I realize quickly I'm not really mad enough at her to want to hurt her.

"No. I'm borrowing her car."

She rallies quickly.

"Be careful driving that monstrosity, Olivia. I don't know why she doesn't trade that behemoth in for a normal car."

"I'll be careful, Mom. Love you."

"We love you, too, sweetheart." Before I can hang up, she adds, "Call your husband, Olivia. He needs to know about the baby."

****

I'm tempted to crawl back in bed, but instead, I put on a loose sundress, one of the few things that still fit, and go downstairs to retrieve the keys to Junie's car.

My mother isn't wrong, the car is a behemoth. A dark green 1976 Cadillac Eldorado convertible with tan leather interior, it is the perfect car for an elderly movie star like Aunt Junie. I'm not sure I can possibly pull off the old world glamour she can behind the wheel, but I back it out of the yard and head north on the overseas highway.

At four months along, almost everything I brought with me is suddenly too snug. It won't be long before I won't be able to wear any of it. I'm overjoyed at the thought of having a baby, but I'm frightened by the proof of my pregnancy, and the prospect of facing the coming months alone.

When I was pregnant with our son, I breathed a sigh of relief when the first trimester was over, foolishly believing that the danger of losing him was over. It never crossed my mind that after listening to my unborn child's sturdy heartbeat for eight months, I'd one day lie there in the obstetrician's office and be greeted by ominous silence.

Perfectly formed, he died in my womb.

****

Exhausted from my shopping trip, I'm sitting on the porch swing drinking an ice-cold soft drink when Dianna joins me that evening.

She has aged in the last few years, but her dark eyes still sparkle with the same intelligence as always. Over the years, I have come to recognize the shadows and sadness within their dark depths but have never known their source.

I scoot over so she can sit beside me on the swing. We sit there in silence for a few minutes.

"I can't seem to get enough sleep," I say after stifling several yawns.

"When I was pregnant with my son, I could have slept all day long."

I look at her in surprise, and she laughs out loud.

"You didn't know I had a son?" she asks. "Of course not, Sylvia was so adamant that Corliss and I were lesbians, I suppose she never brought up the whole truth of the matter, did she? I have a son who lives in Michigan. His name is Edward. Everyone has always called him Eddie. He has a son and a daughter. So not only am I a mother, I'm a grandmother, too."

I'm shocked by this news. I remember Opal's family coming to visit occasionally. For a day or two, Aunt Junie's pool would be full of nieces and nephews. Then they would head north to the theme parks, continuing home to New Jersey from there, and leaving Aunt Junie's oasis quiet once more. In all the visits we made to

Junie's, I don't recall Diana or Corliss ever having any family around.

"Do you ever see them?" I ask.

"No." The sadness in her voice matches the ever-present sadness in her eyes. "He doesn't really care to see me, and his kids don't know me at all."

"Why wouldn't he want to see you and have his kids know you?"

"We came down to Florida in 1965, when Eddie was seven. It was supposed to be some grand family vacation where we would take pictures of us lounging around the hotel pool in the middle of winter and make everyone back home insanely jealous. That's how Ted, my husband, was. He longed to have folks envy him. That's why he married me. I was the homecoming queen, a cheerleader, everything a good, smart girl is supposed to be. I had wonderful parents and a beautiful life there in that little town where I was born. I was seventeen when Ted moved to town, just a few months before I graduated from high school. I still remember how crazy all us girls were about the hunky young stranger pumping gas at Melvin's station. When he started paying me attention, I was overwhelmed. I dropped my nice, upstanding high school sweetheart and started dating him. I got pregnant with Eddie, and we got married. In that order."

"What happened?" I prod when she grows silent.

"He got a good job, started climbing the ladder in his company, and the closer he got to the top, the more miserable he became. He brought his misery home and took it out on me. He broke my ribs, broke my nose, left me black and blue more times than I can count, but I stayed with him because we had a son, and I was desperately afraid of what a custody battle would do to him. Ted was a successful businessman by then. He was young, but it seemed everything he touched turned to gold. The folks in town loved him and never would have believed me if I told them he was beating me.

"When we came down for vacation that year, he was so calm and even-tempered. It was hard to believe he was the same man. And then, the night before we were to go back, he went to the bar down the road from the hotel. When he got back, he was drunk, but not drunk enough to just go to bed and pass out. Instead, he picked a fight with me, then nearly killed me for talking back to him. He packed his and Eddie's bags, took me to the hospital, and left me there in the emergency room. Before he left, he promised me that if I ever tried to contact them, he'd kill Eddie first, and then he'd kill me."

She sniffs back her tears as she pats my hand.

"You've enough going on that you certainly don't need to bear the burdens of a silly old woman."

"Wait," I say as she starts to stand. "Have you ever spoken to your son since then?"

She nods, a wistful smile playing about her mouth.

"He called me after Ted died. We talked for a bit, but we didn't have much to say. Ted had told him I got sick and died on our trip. They relocated to a different town with Ted's job a few months after, and Ted cut off all contact with my family. Eddie never had any reason to doubt his father's words until an aunt told him the truth after Ted's death. Now, he sends me a Christmas card each year, along with a picture of his family. They came down once a few years ago, and we visited at a restaurant in Key Largo. He has a nice wife, and the kids are very polite."

As if wearied by the telling of her story, she leans

her head back and closes her eyes. A moment later, she is snoring softly.

She retired five years ago from the bank where she had worked for as long as I can remember. I knew she started as a teller and moved up to be a loan officer. She was the one person here Mama seemed to admire a little, save for the fact that she may or may not be a lesbian. It never occurred to me that she had a life outside Aunt Junie's house and the bank, a life that had started and ended before we even knew her.

I wonder how she went on after her son was taken from her. How did she live day after day knowing he was in the hands of a man who beat her so viciously? How many tears did she cry, how many nights did she lie awake wondering how he was?

I run my hand over my own stomach. What would I do to save this baby? Would I give it away if I thought it was the best thing for him or her? Would I let my own heart break to keep my child safe? Would I swallow my own pride to give it the life it deserved? Would I give it a father, no matter the cost to me?

Chapter Seven

Daniel

The phone rings, and I grab it, hoping it's Olivia. My heart sinks when I hear my friend and co-worker Earl's booming voice.

"Jules wanted me to call and invite you over for dinner. She's worried about you."

"Yeah, right. She probably wants to poison me." Julie and Olivia have been best friends since they met at a firm picnic twelve years ago. There's no way in hell she's going to let what I've done go by without some sort of repercussion.

"She talked to Livy this morning. Said Livy asked her if she knew about you and Melanie."

"Tell Julie I'll make sure Liv knows she didn't."

"Julie already told her she didn't. Besides, why would Livy ever believe anything you said again?"

His words sting, regardless of the truth of them.

"I think I'll pass on dinner."

"C'mon, Danny boy. Please let Julie have her say. If I can get you here, and she can give you an earful, maybe she'll forgive me for not telling her about Melanie and let me back in our bed. This couch is so damned uncomfortable, and the kids are starting to ask questions."

"For God's sake, don't tell them what's going on!"

I hated the thought of Cam and Haley knowing how badly I'd screwed things up. I certainly didn't want them to know exactly what I'd done.

"They're teenagers, man. They're pretty good at figuring things out themselves, and if they can't, they'll use their imagination. So you may want to run some offensive there."

"So you want me to make sure they know I'm the cheater, not you?"

"Yeah, basically. There's a lot of words like 'homewrecker,' 'liar,' and 'two-timing SOB' being thrown around right now. I don't need them thinking I'm any of those things."

"I'll think about it and let you know."

"Not good enough. She wants you here Saturday night. I'll make sure the kids are here so she can't lay into you too hard."

"Fine," I agree grudgingly. I need to hear from Julie exactly what Olivia said and how she sounded. I need her to assure me my wife is planning on coming home.

"I don't really know how she is," Julie says. As promised, the kids were here for dinner, but they made hasty escapes as soon as they'd wolfed down their food. I brace myself for the attack I know is coming. "She caught you with another woman. How okay could she be?"

I scrub my hand across my face, trying to clear my head. I hoped Julie would tell me Olivia was fine, but I can tell she's as worried as I am.

"What did she say?"

"As little as possible. Of course, she asked if I knew what an idiot you are before she did, and I assured her I didn't." Julie glares at me across the table. "Other than that, she said she didn't know when or if she's coming home. How could you be such an idiot?"

I open my mouth, but she puts up her hand.

"That is a rhetorical question. I swear, if you try to explain to me why you did what you did, I will punch you in the face." She stands up and starts gathering the dishes from the table. "If she doesn't come back, I swear I will never forgive you."

****

It's still light when I leave Earl and Julie's, and I drive through town. I don't know where I'm going until I pull through the wrought iron gates of the cemetery. I stop when I reach a big oak tree whose branches shade the tiny grave I seek, get out of the car, and walk to spot we buried our son.

It's marked by a simple stone with his name engraved above the date of his birth, which was also the day of his death. Then in tiny letters under the date, a quote from the first book Olivia had placed on the nursery shelf—"Sometimes the smallest things take up the most room in your heart." A rotund little bear holding a balloon is etched there beside the words.

Olivia went to the doctor by herself that day. I was working on a major contract with one of our clients and couldn't get away. She assured me it was no big deal. It was just a routine visit and there would be another in two weeks. I would accompany her then. The client was still in my office when she called.

"Daniel," she said breathlessly. "Something's wrong with the baby. They're sending me to the hospital."

Panic like I'd never known shot through me, and I leapt to my feet.

"I'll be right there, Liv," I promised.

I was there, but there was nothing I could do except hold her hand as she delivered our baby.

The change began that day. There was no way to stop it or deny it. Bit by bit we lost ourselves, until finally we lost us altogether.

I am suddenly overwhelmed with memories of us as we'd been before and as we are now. How had it happened? How in the world had I allowed it to happen?

Tears fill my eyes, and I drop to my knees. It's been years since I prayed desperately for anything, but as I kneel there on the ground, I pray for Olivia and me. I can't imagine how else we'll ever find our way back to us.

Chapter Eight

Olivia

Aunt Junie and I are sitting on the edge of the sand watching the sea birds flitting around the shoreline. It isn't crowded today, only a few fishermen and a handful of the ever-present tourists lined up on the pier.

I've been here for three months, and neither of us has done anything but hint at the fact that she's my biological mother. It's so surreal, I'm able to ignore it for long stretches at a time. But we can't possibly ignore it forever. Can we?

I've been here so many times in the past, watching the sun rise and set, feeding the gulls, walking the streets with her, and she's never said a thing. Not even one little inkling of the truth. She's never been overly affectionate, never nosy about my life. She's asked basic questions. How was school? What college was I planning to attend? How was my job? How was Daniel? Even when I was pregnant the first time, even when we lost our child, there was no hint that she was anything more to me than Aunt Junie. There has been ample opportunity. Just as there is ample opportunity now for her to bring it up, but she doesn't.

"Are you going back to him?" she asks out of the blue.

"Maybe." It's as honest an answer as I can give

without putting more thought into it than I want to yet.

"You don't have to, you know. You can stay here with us. Dianna and I will help you raise her."

"Her?"

"Opal told me she's a girl. And Opal is never wrong about it."

Opal no longer lives in Aunt Junie's backyard. She lives in a nursing home in Miami now, and Aunt Junie and Dianna visit her several times a week. They would have taken care of her after she lost her legs to diabetes, but her nephew and his wife insisted she go to a home closer to them.

"I need to go see her," I say. "I feel bad that I haven't."

"Oh, don't worry about that. Opal understands."

"Everyone here understands," I say.

"That's because we've all been broken in one way or another."

"Dianna told me about her husband."

"Ah, yes, what a sorry son of a bitch he was." She takes off the bejeweled sunglasses she'd been wearing and peers out at the ocean. "It seems we all came together to heal. It took us quite a long time to get Dianna to open up and tell us what happened to her. The rest of us were open with our stories. I knew Corliss's and she knew mine when we came here. Harry's was sad, but not a secret. Opal just never fit in anywhere else, so we accepted her as one of our own. Dianna was broken long before any of us met her. Harry found her in a bar on Duval Street, battered and worn, and he brought her home with him. I was furious. I told him he was crazy and that we could all be killed in our sleep. We knew nothing about this woman except that she was obviously a lush on the prowl and maybe she deserved to have the hell beat out of her."

I try to imagine Dianna as Aunt Junie is describing her, but it's nearly impossible to reconcile the dignified woman I've always known with the woman Aunt Junie describes.

"Do you know what Harry said to me?" Aunt Junie asks with a twinkle in her eye.

I shake my head, and she chuckles.

"You sound just like your sister-in-law, Junetta." She mimics Harry perfectly and laughs again. "That was how Harry was. He wasn't afraid to trust people or to try to find the good in them."

Her eyes fill with tears, and she dashes them away. She clears her throat.

"She never remarried, never fell in love?" I ask.

"Over the years, there were plenty of men in Dianna's life. They came from all walks of life, all levels of society. Yet she wanted nothing more from them than the occasional physical relief that men and women give each other."

"What about Corliss?"

Aunt Junie's eyes take on a distant look.

"She was beautiful. The first time I saw her, all I could think of was a porcelain doll in the window of a toy store. She looked so fragile, as if she could break at the harshest touch. But she didn't. Corliss always remained one of the strongest women I knew."

"Were they...lesbians?" I ask, and even to my own ears I sound prudish.

Aunt Junie looks at me sharply.

"Ah," she says with a nod, "now, *you* sound just like my sister-in-law."

I want to protest, but I can't deny it, and a resigned sigh escapes me.

"Your mother is a good woman, Livy, but she can be the most judgmental, wretched creature I know."

I nod, knowing full well what Junie means by that. So long as people play by my mother's rules, all is well, but once they step out of her very strict boundaries, she wants nothing else to do with them.

"She only stood by me all these years because of you. If not for you, she would have cut me out of their lives long ago. And Oliver would have let her because he loves her more than he loves anyone else on earth."

She grows quiet for a minute, and her fingers toy with the necklace at her throat. Today, she is dressed in a pair of brightly printed palazzo pants and a hot pink off-the-shoulder peasant shirt. A matching scarf is tied around her head like a crown, knotted at the side so the ends hang loose at the side of her head.

Her eyes are fastened on the horizon, and I know she isn't seeing the view but rather some distant place and time. Her fingers continue stroking her necklace.

"I wasn't cut out to be a mother, Livy. Truly. I could never have given you the life Oliver and Sylvie were able to give you. You've known me your whole life, sweetheart. Have you ever once, in all those years, thought, 'Aunt Junie should have a baby'? No, you haven't. Until a few weeks ago, you couldn't imagine me as a mother. Now that you know what I am to you, you're thinking how different your life would have been if I'd raised you, what fun you'd have had. One big adventure, right? But you're still not picturing me as a *mother*. Sylvia is and always will be your mother, Livy. She's the one who changed your diapers and made sure you ate.

She's the one who held you when you were sick or afraid. She's the one who was there when you needed discipline. And when you needed unconditional love. I was only a background character. And that's the way I wanted it."

"So you never regretted giving me up?" I ask, surprised at the hurt that knifes through me.

"Maybe I would have if I'd actually given you up and never seen you again. Maybe if I hadn't been so sure you were taken care of, so certain you were loved. Maybe if I hadn't seen how fulfilled Oliver and Sylvie were by being your parents. Maybe if I hadn't been able to love you the way I could. Maybe then I would have regretted it. But as it was, no. I never regretted it for a moment." She pauses. "I couldn't be what you needed, Liv. Not then. Not now."

"How do you know? How do you know what I needed? How do you know what I need now?"

"Because I've been where you are now," she says. "I've been the betrayed wife. I know exactly how it feels to be pregnant and alone."

I remember Junie as she was when I was a child. The word beautiful doesn't begin to describe her. She had been elegant, sophisticated, and drop-dead gorgeous. In the sun, it's easy to see the signs of aging, the wrinkles on her face, the loose skin of her neck and arms, the age spots on her hands. But now, in her late sixties, and despite all her bright clothing and accessorizing, she exudes a peace most of us can only hope to find. And she is still undeniable beautiful.

Who in the world would have cast aside Junetta Darlington?

"My husband, and your father, was Marshall Elkins.

He was the most handsome, charming man I had ever met. Emerald eyes, golden hair, a lion of a man. He was a rising star, on his way up much faster than I was. We met at a party after the premier of a movie he starred in. I think I fell in love with him on sight. The passion and chemistry between us were instantaneous and unbelievable. We married six months after we met. It was a beautiful ceremony. There must have been five hundred people there. I think I have pictures tucked away somewhere. I'll try to find them, if you'd like to see."

She pauses to take a sip of water from a bottle.

"Our life together was ideal. We bought an estate in California, with a sweeping view of the ocean. We threw parties so lavish you can't even begin to imagine. The house would be full of celebrities, politicians—even a few astronauts made an appearance once or twice. Then I found out I was pregnant. I hadn't meant to get pregnant. Neither of us really wanted children at all, but certainly not at that very moment. I had won a starring role in a new movie, my first real headliner."

Another sip of water. I wondered if she wished it were something stronger.

"Our life together began to fall apart almost immediately. I was seven months pregnant when I caught him in bed with a sweet young intern from the movie studio. I was devastated. It was as if my whole world crashed down around me, and there was nothing I could do to fix it."

I'm entranced by the change in her as she speaks. She has always been even-tempered, but now as she remembers that time in her life, her face changes, her tone changes, pink rises in her cheeks and lightning flashes in her eyes.

"I know your mother told you I was divorced. I'll bet anything she left the next part out. After all, it is hardly the G-rated version of betrayal she would have preferred. Life is hardly G-rated, though, is it? That's why all those sugary sweet movies appeal to people like Sylvia. They offer a two-hour break from the X-rated reality of this world."

She brings her legs up and hunches forward, arms wrapped around them and her cheek resting against her knees as she faces me.

"I bought a gun. There weren't cooling-off periods or any such thing required back then. You went in and bought a gun, no questions asked. So that's what I did. I bought a nice, pearl-handled pistol that fit right inside my purse. I don't know what I was thinking. Three decades later, and I still don't know what the hell I was thinking."

She stops and closes her eyes.

"I shot him when they were both coming out of his dressing room the next night. She was young and naïve enough to think men would do what they said they would if you just did what they asked. Poor, dumb little chit. I couldn't shoot her. I actually felt sorry for her."

"You killed him?" I ask in horrified fascination.

"No."

I think she sounds vaguely disappointed. How in the world did my parents keep such a secret from me all these years?

"What happened?" I prod. She can't stop now. I need to hear the rest of it.

"I went to jail. Not for long. The jury decided it was a crime of passion. They were lenient because I was pregnant, and he didn't die. He even spoke on my behalf.

I was out before you were born, and we signed you over to Oliver and Sylvia immediately. I never wanted you to know what sort of nightmare you came from."

"Was that when you left California and moved to Key West?"

"Yes."

"What happened to her? The other woman?" Even as I ask, I wonder why I care. What difference does it make? I'm probably the only betrayed woman in the world who wants to know why her husband chose the woman with whom he betrayed her.

"Ah, Livy, do you really want to know the answer to that? It's the craziest part of the whole story."

I remain silent. Whether I want to know or not isn't really the question. The question is whether she wants to tell me or not.

"Corliss was the other woman," she says after a long silence. "She came to me a few months after I had you. She was pregnant. She had nowhere to go. Her family had disowned her when she went to Hollywood, and Marshall kicked her out the minute he found out she was pregnant."

"Why did she come to you?"

"She always said it was because I didn't shoot her. She said I was the only person she knew who had ever cared if she lived or died."

"What happened to her baby?"

"Dianna and I tried to talk her into giving it up, but she refused to even consider it. She knew having it would make her life difficult, but she had so much love to give. She was ecstatic about being a mother. It nearly killed her when she had a miscarriage a few months later."

My eyes fill with tears as I think of Corliss losing

the baby she wanted so badly.

"So she just stayed here after she lost the baby?"

Junie nods.

"So Corliss and Dianna weren't lesbians?" I ask, but I don't really care for any reason except assurance that my mother is wrong.

She shrugs eloquently before answering.

"No, but what does it matter? They were there for each other. Your mother only sees the outer shell of people, and what she saw when she came here colored her perception of all of us. She saw a bunch of misfits, criminals, sinners, outcasts, living in sin on hell's half-acre. In reality, we weren't anything that dramatic. We were just broken people who came here to find solace and stayed here because together we were closer to whole."

I think of the broken inhabitants of Aunt Junie's world, the world that so mystified and fascinated me as a child. They all seemed so exotic, so far from my own mundane life. Yet here I am now, one of them, a broken person, seeking solace in this eclectic mixture of lives.

"I think I've had enough of this for one day," Aunt Junie says as she pushes to her feet. She reaches down to help me up, and I place my hand in hers. "Good or bad, you know where you came from now."

Hand in hand, we walk back to the house in silence, both of us lost in thoughts of our own.

****

"Why don't you go lie down, Livy?" Aunt Junie says as we enter the house. "It's good for you and the baby to rest as much as possible. I'll get us some lunch together in a little while."

"I'm not hungry right now, so don't worry about me.

I do think I'll take you up on the offer of a nap, though." I hug her gently. "Thank you, Aunt Junie."

I take a cool shower to rinse the sand from my hair and slip into bed naked. The ocean breeze blows through the open veranda doors, lifting the gauzy curtains from the windows and sending a delicious shiver of cool air across the bare sun-kissed skin of my arms and legs. In the distance, thunder rumbles. A storm is blowing in off the ocean. I think about going back down to the water's edge where I can get a closer view of the magnificent display of God's power, but I don't have the energy. Instead, I just stay where I am, feeling the change in the air as the front moves inland.

My mind can barely absorb everything Aunt Junie told me. The name Marshall Elkins isn't one I recognize, and I wonder what became of him after Aunt Junie left Hollywood. I've never heard of him, so I assume his star didn't continue to rise.

Of all the people who lived here, Corliss was probably my favorite. She was the only one who wasn't just a little bit frightening. She was a pretty lady, with white-blond hair and skin so pale it was almost translucent. Her voice was soft and melodic with a warm southern accent. She made jewelry she sold at the sunset celebration and led ghost tours every night when the sun went down. When she was home, she seemed to always be puttering around the yard in baggy overalls and a big straw hat, but I could always picture her in an antebellum dress, hair in ringlets and a fan in her hand. Like the porcelain doll Aunt Junie compared her to.

When I came to visit, Corliss brushed my hair and painted my fingernails before I went to bed. I always asked her to do it, even though I knew it made Mama mad.

"If you want your fingernails painted, you come to me," Mama scolded more than once as she rubbed an acetone-soaked cotton ball around my brightly hued nails.

She was most taken aback when I emerged from Junie's house with my fingernails painted blue. "Fingernails are not supposed to be blue."

"But I like them blue, Mama. It's how Corliss has hers," I argued from my perch on the side of the bathroom sink later that night.

"How many times do I have to tell you not to talk to that woman?"

"She's so nice, though."

"Healthy fingernails are a lovely pink color," she explained as she put away the nail polish remover and led me to the kitchen table. There, she pulled my hand toward her and began applying the seashell pink polish she let me pick out at the drugstore on the way home from Aunt Junie's. "Blue fingernails mean you aren't getting good circulation. It looks like you're dying when your fingernails are blue."

We didn't know at the time that Corliss of the blue fingernails was, in fact, dying. She knew for years, but she didn't tell anyone, not even Dianna, until her illness was so advanced that she had no choice in the matter.

I turned seventeen the year she died. Mama and I were constantly at odds then, and my attending Corliss's funeral was just one more sore-point between us.

After the funeral, which I attended without either of my parents, I returned to Aunt Junie's house with everyone else. We had bid farewell to the last of Corliss's friends and were cleaning up the kitchen when

Dianna called me into Aunt Junie's harem room. A tall, thin man in a dark suit stood beside her, and as soon I entered, he placed an envelope in my hand.

"Corliss left everything she owned to you. It isn't a fortune, but she hoped it would be enough to see you through college and leave you some extra you could use to, as she put it, 'chase your dreams.' She wanted you to have the means to support yourself, should the need ever arise."

Inside the envelope was a checkbook for an account in my name. Stuck to the front flap of the checkbook was a very short note in Corliss's wide feminine hand. "Never let anyone steal your dreams or keep you at their mercy. Use this gift to make sure you can always stand on your own two feet. Love well and love long, Livy darling. And think of me once in a while."

On the day I graduated from college, I painted my fingernails blue.

Chapter Nine

"Opal," Junie says as we enter her room. "You remember Olivia, don't you?"

Opal gives an exasperated sigh.

"Of course I remember Olivia, Junetta. I lost my legs, not my mind."

I can't help but smile at Opal's familiar gruffness. I expected her to be different, old and sickly. But she sits in her wheelchair, her small body tucked amidst a brightly colored shawl and her hair pinned just as high as it has always been.

"Come give an old woman a hug, child!" she demands.

"How are you, Opal?" I ask as I bend down to hug her.

"I'm fine, fine. Don't listen to these two mother hens. They think just because I'm here, I'm sick. I'm not. I just didn't think either of them was in fit enough shape to be lugging me back and forth, here and there. Besides, I've got everything I need right here, and I don't have to fix my own dinner."

"We'd cook for you, Opal, and you know it."

"Junetta, you've eaten nothing but salad, cereal, and cookies since Harry died. And Dianna eats even less of a variety. Salad three meals a day. Give me a break. If I had to eat like that, I'd be dead in a week."

She lays her hand on my belly and smiles softly. "A

beautiful baby girl, with her father's eyes and her mother's smile."

I try to smile, but tears spring to my eyes.

"Let's see what else we can learn." Opal takes my hand and runs her fingers along the lines in my palm.

"I thought you found the Lord," Dianna says from across the room. "You told us you gave up reading palms."

"Hmmpff," Opal answers and continues her study of my hand.

I wait, breathless, for her to say what she sees there.

"I don't have to read palms to know some things," she says as she folds my hand closed and looks up at me. "Don't you worry, Livy. God is going to bless you with your happy ending."

Chapter Ten

I find the vacant studio two days later as I'm
walking along the waterfront on my way home from
church. It's a beautiful Sunday afternoon, and Mallory
Square is bustling with activity. Cruise ship passengers
are disembarking and disappearing through doors
leading to the various souvenir shops. A few performers
are already giving previews of their sunset celebrations.

A man cycles past me with a tiny brown poodle
staring out from a basket on his handlebars. A toddler
holding a plastic pirate sword breaks away from his
mother and rushes headlong toward the water. His father
catches up with him, swings him high over his head, and
settles him on his broad shoulders. The little pirate beams
with happiness from his perch and waves his sword in
the direction he wants to go.

Over the years, I've tried to imagine Daniel and me
with our son as he would be, living and breathing and
growing into a child, but I can never see past the
moments I held his tiny body in my arms and the endless
childless days that followed.

For a moment, I allow myself to believe Opal's
words, which still ring in my ears. In a few hours, the sun
will set over the horizon, closing out another day of my
self-imposed exile on this island, and for the first time in
months, I dare to believe that all will be well.

Giving in to the hope that beats at my heart, I

imagine holding my daughter and looking into her bright eyes. I imagine her growing, running, playing. I imagine myself as a mother, and I can't help but wonder if Daniel will be with me. It's time for me to make a decision. If I'm not going back, I need to take the steps to end my marriage, though the very idea breaks my heart. If I am going back, I need to go. Whatever I decide, I know I need to tell Daniel I'm pregnant.

I turn away from the water's edge determined that when I get to Junie's, I'll call Daniel and tell him about the baby. How I wish things had been different the day I found out I was pregnant. I wanted so badly to tell him the news in person, to see the joy light up his handsome face, but that hadn't happened, and now a phone call will have to do.

I come to a small alley of storefronts. It is somewhat off the beaten path, but still close enough to be easily accessible to the tourists. I stare at the sign advertising that the space on the corner is for rent. The lettering on the front window proclaims the space Coeur Brisé Studios. I press my face to the glass. A gasp escapes me. I walk around from window to window, falling more and more in love. In the center of the large open room is a large metal sculpture, a heart entwined at the bottom, but broken about two feet from the floor—it breaks into two jagged-edged pieces. For years, I've horded the remainder of the money Corliss left me, dreaming of owning an art gallery of my own. I have looked at several places before, but I've never found one that is as perfect as this appears to be.

For the first time since I sent my cell phone to its watery grave, I wish I had it with me. I may not want to talk to my husband, my mother, or even my best friend, but I definitely want to speak to Peter Salazar, the contact listed on the sign. I scribble the number down on a napkin from my purse and hurry home.

Junie looks at me as if I have just sprouted a horn from my head when I tell her I'm thinking of opening a gallery here in Key West.

"Olivia," she says, "perhaps you should give this a bit more thought. This may not be the best time for you to make monumental decisions. Pregnancy can make a woman a bit irrational."

I can't help the laugh that escapes me.

"A bit irrational?" I repeat. "That is quite an understatement from a woman who attempted to murder her husband while she was pregnant."

Junie says nothing as she turns away from me, but I can feel her hurt and anger, and I regret my words immediately.

"I'm sorry," I say.

"Dianna and I are going out to dinner with friends. We'll be home late."

She disappears through the door without another word.

Heedless of her warning, I call Peter Salazar about the space he has for rent.

His voice is deep and slightly accented. He tells me he'll be coming into town from Atlanta on Wednesday afternoon. We make an appointment to meet at six o'clock that night, and as quickly as that, I have taken the first step toward a life without my husband.

****

Over the next four days, I think of calling Daniel a few times, but I quickly push the thought away and go back to my plans for the gallery. I don't want to talk to either Daniel or my parents before I've made my decision. If I do, they'll only try to talk me out of it, and I don't want to hear all their reasons why it isn't a good idea.

Aunt Junie has avoided me since the night I told her about the gallery. I don't really blame her, nor do I mind. I want to be alone with pen and paper, drafting and redrafting my ideas. Suddenly obsessed, I forcefully ignore every twinge of doubt that enters my mind.

On Monday, the phone rings. Aunt Junie and Dianna are visiting Opal, and I try to ignore it, but I am afraid it may be Peter Salazar, and I don't want to miss his call.

"Olivia, I've been worried to death about you," my mother says. "Why haven't you called me?"

"I've been busy," I say.

"Yes, Junetta told me that."

I hear the disapproval in her voice, and I know Junie has betrayed me to my mother.

"Junetta says you're planning to lease some space to open an art gallery. Is that true?"

My blood boils as I wonder which of them called the other. Not that it matters, for here I am, doing what I'm not yet ready to do, talking to my mother about my plans.

"Yes, it's true."

"So you don't plan to come back? You're just going to live down there and raise the baby alone?"

"I'm not alone. You forget my *mother* lives here, too."

I hear her gasp of pain, and I wonder what's wrong with me. I have never been intentionally cruel and yet, the past few months, I can't seem to help myself. There is no chance for me to apologize before she hangs up.

****

I'm standing in the kitchen eating pistachio ice cream out of the carton when Junie and Dianna come through the door.

"Opal sends her love," Junie says without much warmth. Obviously, she is still angry at me.

"My mother called," I say. "Thanks a lot for telling her about my plans."

"Olivia, I'm worried about you. I thought maybe Sylvia could talk some sense into you."

"Perfect. Like one mother wasn't enough." I stalk outside, slamming the door behind me.

I go to the pool that separates the main house from the three small bungalows. I sit down on the edge and dangle my feet in the water. Plants fill the yard and tropical birds call to each other from within their leaves and branches. A large iguana suns itself near the back corner of the fence, and I fight the quick flutter of nervousness I always feel when I notice one of the spiked creatures that populate the island.

When Daniel and I last visited, he chased a smaller one down and caught it. I'm still not sure how. I refused to watch, certain he was about to lose a finger or toe, or at the very least, suffer a nasty, germy bite. There is a picture in our living room of him holding the thing up, smiling proudly.

I wonder if the pictures are still in their places or if Daniel has taken them down and put them away. Julie swore he hasn't been with Melanie since I left, but I can't help wondering if she is there in our house with him. I feel sick at the thought.

Chapter Eleven

Daniel

The rain that began earlier in the day hasn't let up a bit as I eat supper at the kitchen sink. If I keep eating fast food every night, Olivia won't have to divorce me. I'll be dead of clogged arteries before she even calls to tell me.

I'm throwing away the trash when someone knocks at the door. I open it to find my father-in-law standing there. Dooley peers out from the top of his raincoat.

"Oliver! Come in. What in the world are you doing out in this weather? Is everything all right?"

He doesn't say anything as he puts Dooley on the floor, takes off his raincoat, and hangs it on the rack by the front door. The dog makes a mad dash for the sliding glass door that leads to our small patio and begins sniffing wildly. His owner's gait is slower, less certain as he moves toward the easy chair he always frequents when he and Sylvia visit.

"Want a drink?" I ask as I follow him. I want one with a passion, but he shakes his head and motions for me to sit on the sofa.

"Sit down, son."

I do so without question while my stomach clenches with dread. I remember the last time he and Dooley showed up at my door unexpectedly.

****

Olivia and I had been dating nearly a year when someone knocked on my apartment door. When I opened it, Oliver was standing there, a solemn look on his face. I let him in, quickly cleaning off a space on the worn plaid sofa my roommate and I shared.

I had met him and Sylvia before, because Olivia was insistent that we meet sooner rather than later. I still think it was just her excuse to give me somewhere to go for Thanksgiving, but I didn't look a gift horse in the mouth. With no family to my name after the death of my aunt the year before, I had nowhere else to go. Since then, I'd been a pretty constant presence at their house.

"Can I help you, Mr. Darlington?" I asked.

"I hope so," he answered. "I need you to answer a question for me."

I swallowed nervously, waiting for the question.

"What are your intentions toward my daughter?"

"My what, sir?"

"Your intentions. You've been seeing her for quite a while now, and I'd like to know why you keep seeing her."

Why? I thought wildly. What was the right answer to that? I could tell him it was because she was sexy as hell, but I doubted he wanted to hear that. I could say it was because she made me laugh or because she was the smartest, sweetest girl I ever met. I wasn't sure what he wanted to hear, so I just said what I knew.

"Because she's Olivia, sir. She's different from anyone else I've ever met. You know her, Mr. Darlington. You know all the things that make her special. But if I had to summarize why I love her in one sentence, I'd say it's just who she is and who I am when

I'm with her. She makes me, *me*, sir. I love her. And I can't imagine how I'd ever live without her."

When I was done with my somewhat bumbling and awkward explanation, he smiled and stood up. Holding out a hand, he shook mine firmly.

"That's all I need to know."

****

Now, all these years later, I sit here feeling just as nervous as I did then.

"Is Sylvia all right, Oliver?" I ask as he continues to study me.

"Sylvia's fine, son."

"And you? Everything's all right with you?"

He inclines his head slightly, and the nervousness takes on an edge of panic.

"Olivia?" I don't even know how to phrase the horrible fears that leap to mind.

His eyes meet mine, and I swallow a lump in my throat. His eyes are bleak and worried, and I fight the urge to grab him by the collar and force the words out of his mouth.

"What are your intentions toward my daughter?"

"What?" I blink at him. I've always appreciated his wry sense of humor, but I'm not sure that's what this is.

"Your intentions toward my daughter, Daniel. What do you intend to do about her?"

"I don't know, Oliver. I think it's up to Olivia at this point. I've called her. I've apologized. Now, it's up to her to decide if she's coming home or not."

He stands up slowly, his face somber. I wait for his outstretched hand, but it doesn't come. He scoops Dooley up and heads toward the door without a word. As he finishes buttoning his coat, he looks at me again.

"I never thought you'd give her up so willingly, or I wouldn't have let you have her."

He is through the door before I can say anything in return.

I listen as his car pulls out of the driveway. Then I go to the kitchen shelf that recently became my liquor cabinet and take out the half-empty bottle of whiskey. I ignore the makings of a mixed drink, and instead bring the bottle to my lips.

Because one gulp of whiskey can't possibly help me silence Oliver's words, I take the bottle with me to my recliner in front of the television, prop my feet up, and turn it on. There is nothing on I want to watch, so I switch to the channel that plays classic rock. When Olivia is cleaning the house, this is the music she listens to. One of my favorite things is walking in on her dancing to some song from our youth as she vacuums or dusts. She always laughs when I tell her how sexy she is, because she knows as well as I do that she doesn't have a single ounce of rhythm. Still, my body responds to the sway of her hips the same as it did when we were nineteen.

I want her back so badly I can barely stand it, but I'm not sure what Oliver expects me to do. I can't make her forgive me. I can't make her come home. Hell, I can't even make her talk to me on the telephone.

I've called a hundred times, but invariably Junie or Dianna answer, and invariably I'm told Olivia isn't in. What I want to ask them is where the hell she is and whether she ever intends to come home. Instead, I leave her be, knowing they're only protecting her. It breaks my heart that they're protecting her from me.

The phone rings, and I quickly grab it, still hoping every time it rings that Olivia is calling to tell me she's coming home. I groan when I hear Sylvia's voice.

"Are you planning to go get her?" she demands without an introduction.

"No," I answer. I figured she was behind Oliver's surprise visit.

"Why not?"

"Sylvia, I'll tell you the same thing I told Oliver. If Olivia wants to come home, she'll come home. If she doesn't, I can't make her."

"Of course she wants to come home. Daniel, for goodness' sake. You need to make more of an effort. You made this mess, and it's up to you to clean it up. You're the one with work to do, not Olivia."

I grudgingly admit to myself that she's right. It is my mess. Maybe I haven't made it clear to Olivia how sorry I am and how much I want her to come home. Maybe if I go there in person, I can make her understand.

"Fine," I say, taking another swig of whiskey.

"Are you drinking?" the witch who is my mother-in-law asks.

"Yes, Sylvia, I'm drinking. Why?"

I try to prepare myself for the lecture I know is coming. Her words when she finally speaks are unexpected.

"She's talking about opening a gallery down there, you know."

"What?" The world darkens around me. Olivia has always dreamed of owning an art gallery. She's looked at several places here in the city, but she's never found the right spot. How could she have found it hundreds of miles from home?

"Are you going after her?" Sylvia demands again.

"Yes," I say, because I have no choice. My wife is

making a life without me. I need to at least try to stop her.

Chapter Twelve

Olivia

I dress carefully for my meeting with Peter Salazar.
I want to make a good impression, after all.

The dress I choose is a blue halter dress with an
empire waist. It flares out just under my breasts and there
is enough material to conceal the rounding of my belly
beneath it. It's a beautiful ocean blue that shows off the
tan I've acquired. I add a pair of low-heeled sandals and
a beaded bracelet the same shade as my dress. and paint
my lips a light glossy pink. A bit of mascara and I'm
done.

I arrive at the gallery at six on the dot and knock on
the door.

When the door opens, I am immediately struck by
the man's handsomeness. Mesmerizing blue eyes stare
into mine, and my breath catches in my throat.

"Mrs. Carson? I'm Peter Salazar. Come in." He
motions me into the gallery as I try to place his slight
accent.

He talks as I follow him through the lower room, and
I find myself lost in the deep cadence of his voice.

Though the gallery is lit only by dim wall sconces at
the moment, I can imagine how the sunlight will pour
through the windows during the day. The lighting
already installed will provide perfect illumination for

nighttime events.

The heart sculpture is illuminated with pink and blue lights that shine from its center. It isn't enough light to touch anything except the jagged edges of the broken halves, which I can now see are covered in bits of mirrored glass that reflect the light like a million little stars. It is a beautiful display.

"Coeur Brisé," he says when I stop to study it. "Broken heart."

My own broken heart skips a beat. This is the perfect place for me.

He leads me upstairs to the apartment above. An open-floor-plan living area is separated from the kitchen by a granite-topped island. From the vast expanse of windows that make up one wall of the room, I can see the people making their way to the waterfront. This is a prime location.

"This is the master bedroom and bath," he says, pushing open a door to show me an elegant bedroom and a generous bath. "And there is a smaller room here."

He opens the door to a room with soft peach walls, and I sigh happily. This would make the perfect nursery.

Disappointment flows through me. We haven't even discussed the price, but I know there's no way I can afford such a gorgeous, perfect place.

"It's wonderful, Mr. Salazar," I say as he leads the way back downstairs. "I'm sorry I wasted your time. I didn't realize how large and well-placed it is until now."

"Please, call me Peter. And forgive me for not understanding, but those don't seem like reasons to turn it down. Does it not fit your needs? Do you not like it?"

A small laugh escapes me. "Oh, it more than fits my needs. It's perfect. Too perfect for me to afford."

"Ah, I see. But, we haven't even discussed the terms, Mrs. Carson. It may not be as hopeless as you think. I believe we can work out something acceptable to both of us."

"Really?" I ask breathlessly, afraid to hope he's right.

"Of course."

"Olivia," I blurt out. "Please call me Olivia."

I can barely control my excitement, and his smile tells me he knows this.

"Okay, Olivia." He places a hand at my back and turns me to the door. "Let's talk over supper. I'm famished."

Finding a quiet restaurant near Mallory Square at sunset is nearly impossible, so I agree when he suggests we eat in the restaurant at his hotel. I follow him through the lobby to the waterfront restaurant. It isn't very crowded, but he asks the pretty blonde hostess for as private a table as possible.

"Of course, Mr. Salazar. Follow me." She leads us past the bar and up the stairs to a small private deck. Unlike the tables downstairs, the two tables here are covered with tablecloths, and candles flicker in the wrought iron lanterns set in the centers of them. "Will this do?"

"Yes, Hillary, thank you." He presses a tip into her hand, and she smiles her thanks at him, an unspoken invitation in her eyes.

"The gallery space belonged to my wife," he explains after we order. "Paulina loved it. She loved the location, the building. She loved Key West more than any place on earth. Personally, I've never seen the attraction."

I smile. Daniel feels the same way. He sometimes agrees to vacation in the Keys, because he loves fishing and diving, but he couldn't care less about visiting Key West itself, much less living here. I, on the other hand, love it. Its rich history and sense of casual hedonism speak to me on a level I have never fully explored. I wonder now if it's something I inherited from Junie.

"She wanted to be here always. Every day, every night. She didn't care if anyone ever came in to look at anything she displayed, so long as they walked past her window. She wanted to see them more than she wanted them to see her."

I notice he speaks of her in the past tense, and I want to ask why, but I don't.

He continues. "As I was giving you the tour, I realized I can't part with the gallery. Not permanently. Not yet. My family will think I'm crazy. They say I should sell it and get on with my life, but I can't seem to do that." He shakes his head sadly. "Tell me, Olivia, how does one get on with a life that has been unbelievably, irreparably damaged?"

His question hits so close to home I don't trust myself to speak, so I shrug helplessly. Moved by the pain in his eyes, I cover one of his hands with my own.

He clears his throat as the waiter brings our food.

"What brings you here? Looking to change your life so drastically?" he asks, eyeing the thin silver band that still encircles my finger. "And what does your husband think of such a change?"

I don't know what it is about him that makes me blurt out the whole sordid story of my life. As if my mouth has a mind of its own, it opens, and everything just tumbles out. By the time I stop talking, he knows about Aunt Junie, Daniel, and the baby. He knows it all.

I wait for him to run.

I wait for him to tell me he would never let a crazy person have his beloved Paulina's art gallery.

He has been leaning forward, listening to every word, and now he leans back in his chair. He studies me silently, without moving any part of himself except his eyes.

Nervous and embarrassed, I take a big gulp of my water. Then I reach for my purse. I've ruined any chance I had to lease the space, and there's no need to prolong the inevitable.

"I'm so sorry," I say. "I don't know why I just told you all that."

He lays his hand over mine to still me.

"Don't leave," he says. "It's all right."

I shake my head.

"No, it's not. I have better manners than that. I really do. You must think I'm a total idiot."

"Stop," he says. "Sometimes, things have to come out. I don't mind. Really. Actually, it helped me make up my mind."

"Great." I groan. If he's made his mind up based on that crazed discourse, then he's certainly decided against having anything more to do with me.

His laughter is warm and rich, without a hint of maliciousness.

"I've decided I don't wish to lease the studio." He leans forward again, his eyes boring into mine. "I've decided I want to be a part of anything opened there. I would like to hire you to run the gallery. You will have free rein except for two things. The name must stay the same. And I am free to arrange exhibits for artists I find."

Although this isn't quite what I had in mind, it is perfect for now. Still, it won't be quite the same as owning my own gallery.

"I've just come up with this idea sitting here, so I'm not sure of its feasibility. It may prove to be too painful to be there in Paulina's world without her. If that is the case, I will give you first option to buy or lease it, and I will give you a price you can afford. You may decide to go home, and I will let you out of our agreement without repercussions."

"Really?" I can hardly contain my excitement.

"Really," he says with a smile. "You will be perfect there."

I readily agree to his proposal, trying not to think of the opposition I am sure to meet from my family or how permanently this will separate me from the life I've left behind.

"Would you like to walk along the pier?" he asks as we leave the restaurant. "Paulina and I found truly talented artists at festivals and places such as this. I haven't been here in a while. Perhaps there's someone new."

When we come to a man selling landscapes, we both stop to admire his talent. They are excellently done, and as I enjoy their beauty, Peter keeps up a low conversation with the man. Finally, he hands him his card.

"He is a very talented artist. His first time here. Quite serendipitous.I told him to call us to arrange a showing."

He places his hand on the small of my back, and I can feel his thumb on the bare skin at my waistline. I know I should move away from him, but instead, I let him guide me along. As we walk, he tells me about his import business in Atlanta and his children, Adele and Marc.

The toe of my sandal catches on something and I stumble. His arms come around me quickly, catching me before I fall.

"Careful," he warns softly against my ear and an unexpected shiver of desire shoots through me.

Shocked by my reaction, I quickly step away. He lets me go without protest, but I see the answering response in his eyes.

"Paulina and I were married for eighteen years," he tells me. "She was killed in a car accident two years ago. It was late and raining. She lost control of the car. She crossed the median and hit a truck head-on. I thought of moving here and running the studio, but our lives, mine and the children's, are in Atlanta. It seemed too cruel to make them leave their schools and their friends to move here."

"Did she live here?"

"Yes," his voice holds a wealth of regret, so I don't prod him for answers to the questions swirling through my head.

He stops and looks at me for a long moment. His eyes take me in from head to toe, and I can see the attraction there. And the fear that I'm sure echoes my own.

"I think it's time to say goodnight, Olivia."

Chapter Thirteen

Daniel

I drive to Key West the day after Oliver's visit. I have a relentless hangover, and I'm exhausted from lack of sleep, but I make it in one piece and go straight to Junie's.

"Daniel," Junie says coldly when she opens the door.

"I need to talk to Olivia."

"She isn't here."

"Where is she?"

Her eloquent shrug says a lot about the starlet she must have been in her heyday.

"I have no idea where she is, Daniel, but I'll be happy to tell her you stopped by."

She tries to push the door closed, but I hold it open. I wouldn't usually use brute strength against a helpless old lady, but I know Junie too well to think she's helpless. Besides, I've just about had it with the dragons guarding Olivia. I intend to see her, no matter how much fire they breathe.

"I didn't just stop by, Junie. I drove all day to get here. Now, tell me where my wife is."

"Fine. I'll tell you. She's at the gallery. The owner is showing it to her tonight."

"Tonight? Why tonight? Don't people usually show

real estate in the daytime?"

Her laugh is uncharacteristically haughty.

"Not always, darling. He and Olivia thought it best they meet tonight."

"Where is it?"

"Where they all are. A few blocks from Mallory Square, off Duval. It's Coeur Brisé Studios. If they aren't there, look around a bit. They may have decided to stop for a bite to eat."

I growl out a thank you and head in the direction of the waterfront.

Finding a place to park is torturous, and by the time I find the gallery, the lights are all out and there's no sign of my wife or the man she's with.

Knowing how Olivia loves walking along the waterfront this time of night, I decide to look for her there. As I walk, I wonder how safe it is for her to meet with a strange man at night. The news is full of rapists and killers who use the classified ads to lure unsuspecting victims. I find it hard to believe that Junie and Dianna would let Olivia wander the streets alone at night, much less meet a stranger in an empty studio after dark. The thought occurs to me that maybe he isn't a stranger just as I see her exit the hotel doors.

She looks gorgeous, and for a few minutes, I simply drink in the sight of her. Her skin is tanned, and her dark hair has been subtly lightened by the sun. The dress she's wearing accentuates her breasts and shows a great deal of her back and I wonder what she was thinking when she chose it.

She points toward a table full of paintings, and it's then I notice the man beside her. An indulgent smile creases his face as he follows her to the display that's captured her attention. She searches the tables, picking up various paintings, while the man and the artist speak earnestly. As she moves about the tables, I catch glimpses of her face. She is absolutely glowing, and I want nothing more than to take her in my arms and kiss her senseless. I start toward her, but before I can reach her, the man hands the artist a business card, and he and Olivia walk away.

I'm near enough now that I can call out to her, and I open my mouth to do so, but it snaps shut as the man's hand comes to rest possessively on the small of her back. I wait for her to shrug him off or move away, but she stays as she is, letting him guide her through the crowd as I once did.

Rage like I have never known stops me in my tracks. I want to kill the man who has taken my place at her side. He has no business touching her back, no business listening to her talk, or looking into her eyes.

Suddenly, she stumbles over some unseen obstacle, and I jerk toward her, but the stranger catches her, his arms encircling her protectively. She laughs at herself as she always does, and I recognize the bemused wonder on his face.

In that moment, as I savor the familiar strains of Olivia's laughter, I know I've lost her, or as Oliver said, I've let her go. I stumble back through the crowd and into the nearest bar, where I spend the rest of the night trying to drown the memory of Olivia in love.

****

I wake up the next afternoon in a hotel room I don't remember renting, still dressed in last night's clothes.

"So you're awake?" a woman says from across the room. I open one eye and stare hard at Dianna.

"How'd I get here?"

"I had a couple of strong young men carry you in. Don't worry, they enjoyed it more than you did." She laughs, a hyena-like sound, that makes me want to throw something at her, but there isn't anything in the room that would do the kind of damage I'd like to do.

"How'd you know where I was?"

"You got drunk enough to tell your pathetic story to several people and demand the band keep playing the same sappy country song about a woman looking good in love. When the bartender got ready to rid himself of you, he called us to come get you. He's been a friend for quite some time."

By the time she quits talking, I realize I don't really care how she knew. I just want her to go away and leave me alone. If I can muster up the strength, I fully intend to make my way back to the bar and continue my efforts to drink myself into oblivion. Apparently, I didn't drink nearly enough last night, because I can still see Olivia's tanned shoulders peeking through her dark curls and her laughter is still echoing through my mind.

"Go away, Dianna!" I growl as I cover my face with the pillow.

She snatches it out of my hands and throws it across the room.

"Did you break it off with that woman?" she demands.

"Yes."

"Why?"

"You know why."

"Tell me anyway."

"I love Olivia."

"That isn't a good enough reason. Obviously, you

can't make up your mind who you love. You loved Olivia, then you loved what's-her-name, then you didn't love her anymore, and now you love Olivia again."

"I never loved Melanie."

"Wanted, then. You wanted Olivia, then you wanted what's-her-name. Now you're back to wanting Olivia again. But Olivia deserves better than you just suddenly deciding you want her again. So come up with a better reason why you aren't doing what you were doing with that woman anymore."

I may be stupid, but it doesn't take me long to come up with the reason. Any attraction I ever felt for Melanie is overshadowed by the pain I caused Olivia. There isn't anything or anyone in this world worth what I did to my wife.

But I'll be damned if I'm explaining all that to some dried-up old woman who doesn't have any business asking in the first place.

"Go away. I'm not playing this game with you. Go back and tell Junie I'm going home. Olivia's doing fine without me. She's doing better than fine. She appears to be having the time of her life."

"You really are an ass, Daniel." she proclaims. Then she adds, before leaving me alone in the room, "And a dumb one to boot."

That afternoon, I drive home as I drove down, in one long, tiring ride, and when I fall into our bed, I bury my face in Olivia's pillow in a futile search for a faint remainder of her scent.

I wish I hadn't gone looking for her. Before last night, I could still cling to the image of how she was the last few years, but as I stood back and watched her from a distance, I saw only the girl I fell in love with. It was a strange twist of fate that she came back only after Olivia left me.

Chapter Fourteen

Olivia

"Olivia, are you sure about this?" Aunt Junie asks as she stands in the middle of the studio a week after my first meeting with Peter.

I'm surprised and more than a little irked by her lingering skepticism. Of all the people in the world, I thought she would understand my decision. Stark disapproval is stamped on her face, and my temper rises.

"Yes, I'm very sure," I say stubbornly.

There are doubts, of course. I realize this is a huge step, and although I've prayed repeatedly about it, I have yet to get any real answer to whether it's the right thing to do. I am not, however, going to let that stop me. If the Lord isn't going to show me outright that it's not what I should do, then I'm just going to assume it is. I realize I'm committing to staying here. I'm committing to raising my child here, far away from her father and her grandparents. I'm committing myself to living with my parents' disapproval and my husband's absence.

So why am I able to commit to this, but unable to commit myself to finding an attorney and filing for divorce? In essence, taking Peter's offer says I'm not going back to Daniel. I know that, but I still find it impossible to take that final step that will separate us permanently.

If he gave me any inkling that he still wanted me back, would I even be considering this? I'm not sure of my answer, because Daniel has made no effort to reconcile other than the one measly phone call a month after I left him.

"Olivia, really, perhaps you should think this over some more. Talk it over with your parents, Daniel, someone. I don't think you realize what you're doing."

"I do realize what I'm doing!" I cry. "Daniel isn't here. My parents aren't here. I'm here and you're here and I'm trying to talk it over with you."

"No, you're not. You're trying to talk me over to your side. I don't think I like the idea of you getting mixed up in running this place. You're pregnant. You're hurt. You can't possibly be thinking straight enough to make this kind of commitment. You don't even know this Peter person."

"I don't need you to judge me, Aunt Junie! You gave your baby away! Why? Because you couldn't commit to being a mother? And now you want to talk me out of being able to commit to something? I'm not you, Junetta! I'm nothing like you!"

Silently, she gathers up her things.

"You're right, Olivia. You're nothing like me. I was never a coward who ran away when things got too tough. I faced what had to be done, even if I didn't like it. And my situation was nothing like yours. I lost everything. My husband, my career, my home, everything. Even if I hadn't shot him, Marshall was on his way out the door the moment he found out I was pregnant. You have a husband who loves you and wants to raise a child with you. You have a life you can return to, while the rest of us never had any hope at all of finding what we lost."

She is gone before I can form an appropriate response.

I wander from room to room, futilely trying to find the peace I found the first time I came through the doors. Finally, I give up. I am locking up when the sky lets loose a torrent of rain.

"Wonderful," I mutter as I fight to get my umbrella out of my bag.

"What are you doing?" Peter calls as he rushes up beside me and shields me with his umbrella.

"Drowning," I grumble as my umbrella pops out of my bag and springs open.

He unlocks the door again, and gently pulls me back inside out of the rain. A sound of dismay escapes me.

"What's wrong?"

"Open umbrellas inside are bad luck!" I exclaim as I fight to close it.

"Opening an umbrella inside is bad luck," he corrects.

"Whichever. I don't need to take any chances. My luck's bad enough as it is."

"What's wrong?" he asks again.

"I really need to get home." I'm not in the mood to talk to anyone, and I tell him so.

"Fine," he says. "We won't talk. Just sit here with me while we wait for the rain to slack up."

"I don't think that's a good idea." I'm afraid of how alone and vulnerable I feel. Sitting here with a man I hardly know but am undeniably attracted to isn't a good idea, and I know it.

"Please," he says just as a huge bolt of lightning lights up the sky outside. It seems I have no choice but to wait out the storm.

He looks tired, and I wonder what brought him out on such a horrendous afternoon.

"Why are you here?" I ask.

He gives a bitter bark of laughter.

"Ghosts," he says. "They're everywhere in this town."

I slowly sit down beside him, and when he lifts his arm in invitation, I hesitate only a moment, before I move so that I rest in the crook of it. I don't let myself think about the right or wrong of it, I just accept the comfort and warmth he offers.

"Some days, no matter where I look, all I see are memories," he says.

"Then why come here, of all places?" I ask.

He shrugs. "Maybe it helps to face it head on sometimes. Why are you here?"

"I brought Aunt Junie to see the gallery, but we had a huge fight, and she left."

"I suppose your whole family must think it's a bad idea."

"Of course, but I didn't expect Aunt Junie to. She accused me of running away when things got hard."

He brushes his fingers through my hair, and I like the feel of it far too much.

"Isn't that what you're doing?" he asks quietly.

"I don't know. I didn't think I was running away. I thought I was being strong and independent, showing Daniel and my parents that I could have a life without them."

"Do you think you have that right?"

"What right?"

He put his hand on my belly. "Do you have the right to create a life without them, and in doing that, make your child have a life without them? Do you have the right to make them live a life without this child?"

As I'm prone to do these days, I begin to cry, and he gathers me closer. He wipes my tears away, and when his lips find mine, I don't fight it. His hand rests against my cheek and his fingers stroke the strands of hair that fall across them.

A flicker of desire springs to life inside me. My hand travels to his chest, where I can feel his heart beating rapidly.

"Olivia," he whispers against my mouth. I move closer, losing myself for a moment in the gentle insistence of his mouth, his touch.

Our kiss deepens, his hand brushes against my breast, and he leans forward, gently pushing me back. For a moment, I let my body follow his lead.

"Let me make love to you."

I'm tempted to give in, tempted to find in him the passion I so envied in my husband's eyes. Maybe one day I will, but not today.

"I can't," I say against his mouth. "I'm sorry."

He pulls back slowly, reluctantly.

"It's okay," he says as I apologize again. "It's too soon. I shouldn't have pushed you. I'm the one who should apologize."

I want to touch him, offer him some reciprocal comfort to make the sadness within him disappear, but I don't think it will do any good now. The spell is broken for the moment, and we are just two sad and lonely people who aren't ready yet to say good-bye to our ghosts.

"You have nothing to apologize for," I assure him. "I wanted it as much as you did. But I'm married. I can't cheat on Daniel. And I can't let you think this can be anything more than what it is."

"Are you going back to him, then?"

"I don't know," I admit. "Not yet."

"Does he want you back?"

"He tells people he does, but he hasn't told me. Well, that's not quite right. He called me once and asked me to come back. But he's never called again. It's been months."

He sighs in resignation.

"But you'll keep waiting?"

"No," I say quietly, and the tears threaten again. "I can't wait forever."

"Neither can I," he says as he stands up and offers me his hand. "But I'll wait as long as I can."

Chapter Fifteen

I'm at the studio early the next morning when Peter comes through the door with two cups of coffee and a brown paper bag.

My heart flutters with nervousness as I remember yesterday afternoon. I wish I could blame my hormones for my enthusiastic response to him, but I can't lie to myself. It might have been a while since I felt it, but I know exactly what it was.

"I brought us some breakfast," he says, holding the bag aloft while I try not to meet his gaze.

I follow him to the kitchen and pull out a paper-wrapped bundle from the bag. The fragrant steam from the Danish makes my stomach growl.

"You need to eat more," he admonishes with a gentle touch of his lips to the top of my head. I know I should discourage his continued familiarity, but I remain silent instead. "The baby needs extra."

"I eat. Believe me, I eat. I just didn't think about it this morning."

Neither of us mentions what happened between us as we devour the pastries.

"Did I tell you that my children are coming into town today?" he asks, and I shake my head. "Paulina's parents are bringing them down. They have them three weeks during the summer and my parents have them for three weeks. They come home to me for two weeks in between. It was the way we did it when she was alive. It gives them a chance to know their grandparents well. I didn't want to stop it after she died."

"What time should they arrive?"

"Around two. Their flight arrives in Miami at ten. I told them to meet me here at the gallery."

"Will coming here upset them?"

"Who? Her parents or the children?"

"Both. Either."

"I don't think so. Besides, I want them to meet you, and I don't think I could talk you into coming to my hotel room."

"No," I agree. "You couldn't."

We stay busy the rest of the morning and before we realize it, there is a sharp rap at the door followed by the sounds of children.

"Daddy!" cries a dark-haired little girl as she leaps into his arms.

"Adele my belle!" he exclaims and swings her around. She giggles and buries her face in his neck.

"I missed you."

"And I missed you." He sets her down and turns to the boy, who hangs back a little. Clearly, he considers himself at an age when it's no longer acceptable for a boy to plow into his father's arms.

"Hello, son," Peter says, taking a step toward him. "I've missed you, too."

They wrap their arms around each other, and the tears that hover so near my surface clog my throat. It is always this way when I see a boy and his father. How I wish I could have given that gift to Daniel.

"You've grown a foot since I last saw you," Peter declares as he steps back.

"It's only been a month, Dad," the boy says. He sends me a curious glance.

Peter hugs his in-laws, who are also looking at me with interest. When all the greetings are out of the way, he pulls me toward them.

"This is Olivia. She's re-opening the studio for me."

"It was our mother's," Adele says primly.

"Yes, I know," I say with a smile.

"She was beautiful." This comes from Marc who has moved away from Peter and gone to stand beside his grandmother. "More beautiful than you."

"Skinnier, too," Adele adds helpfully.

As uncomfortable as I feel, her words make me laugh.

"Olivia's having a baby," Peter informs her, and my unease grows.

Paulina's mother makes a little noise of distress, and her husband quickly bends near her, speaking softly in a language I don't know.

The children are staring at my belly with mounting horror in their wide dark eyes.

My gaze swings to Peter, who is looking at me with mild amusement, obviously in no hurry to clear up their misunderstanding.

"My husband and I are very excited," I say, running my left hand over my stomach so that they can see the ring on my finger.

"Wonderful!" Paulina's father exclaims, and his wife beams at me. "Congratulations."

"Is it a girl or a boy?" Adele asks.

"I don't really know yet, but I think it's a girl."

"What will you name her?"

"Ava," I say, remembering the day Daniel and I

agreed on that name. I was three weeks late and we were certain I was pregnant. We decided on Ava for a girl and that choice never wavered, even when my period came two days later, and we had to start dreaming all over again.

"What if it's a boy?" Marc asks.

"I don't know yet," I say.

"The first son should be named for his father," Paulina's mother says.

I close my eyes against the crushing pain as I see the name engraved on a tiny headstone. Daniel Oliver Carson was named for the father and grandfather he never knew.

"I'd better get home. It was nice meeting you all." I try to smile but find it too difficult. I rush through the door, ignoring Peter as he tries to stop me.

I don't go straight home. I walk around town. I wander through the Audubon House and Garden. I stop in a shop and buy a dozen white daisies. Then I walk through the cemetery, looking for the graves of infants and placing a flower on each of their headstones. It's a rather morbid pastime I've taken up the last few years.

The sun is setting as I place the last flower. I think about going to Mallory Square, but I'm afraid I'll run into Peter and his family. That's the last thing I want to do right now.

****

Aunt Junie is in her harem room waiting for me when I walk through the front door.

"Olivia, come here," she commands, and I obey without question.

The room still reeks of decades-old marijuana smoke. Aunt Junie lounges on one of the large pillows, dressed in a kimono of blue silk threaded with gold and silver. A blue turban covers her hair and small silver hoops dangle from her ears.

"Sit down," she orders when I stand there in the doorway. Wondering what this is about, I do as I'm told. She hardly waits for me to settle myself on the settee before she starts talking. "I refuse to talk to you as your mother, because you have a mother, and I'm not her. So I will talk to you as your aunt and friend. As your aunt and friend, I think it's my place to warn you if I see you doing something akin to jumping off a cliff. Don't you agree?"

"Yes," I say begrudgingly. "But why do you see my opening the studio that way? I thought you wanted me to stay here."

"I do, darling. I want you and the baby and maybe even Daniel to be here. But I want you to be happy."

"I am happy, Aunt Junie. I have the baby. I'm going to have the studio. I'm happy."

"Did I ever tell you about Harry?"

The sudden change in subject worries me for a moment, but she doesn't wait for me to speak.

"He kept a picture of his wife on his dresser in our room until the day he died."

I make some sound of surprise, and she smiles sadly.

"You thought I was the love of his life," she surmises. "I suppose everyone did. But I wasn't. Truthfully, I was never even close to being the love of his life. I knew that from the day I met him, and he never tried to convince me otherwise. He and Margaret met in elementary school. He always said he asked her to marry him the day they met. Of course, they were only six years old, so they had to wait a while."

She chuckles lovingly.

"They married when they were fifteen. They had three children and eight grandchildren. She was always a housewife. She cooked and cleaned and took care of his every need, while he taught high school English to a bunch of hooligans. He told me some days it was only the thought of going home to her that got him through the day. At night, they both chased their dreams. For over thirty-five years, they spent two hours every night following their dreams. He wrote his books and she illustrated them. They had over a dozen published."

She twists the ruby ring on her left hand. She's worn it as long as I can remember, and I've always known it was a gift from Harry.

"Their children grew up and moved away, and Harry and Margaret were able to give more and more of their time to each other and their talents. They were invited to a party for their publishing house. Margaret didn't want to go, but Harry thought it would be good for them to go. He insisted, and she gave in. He promised Margaret they wouldn't stay long, and even though they were enjoying themselves, he kept his promise and they left early. It was dark and Harry was behind the wheel. As they came up on a bridge that crossed a swift-moving creek, he looked out at the water. He missed seeing the deer before it was right in front of them. He swerved trying to miss it, and lost control of the car. It spun across the road, flipped over, and rolled down an embankment. It landed upside down in the water. Harry was able to get out, but Margaret's side of the car was crumpled, pinning her inside."

"Oh, how horrible!" I cry. "I had no idea he was a widower."

"He wasn't. Not really. Margaret was in a vegetative state for twenty-five years. I met Harry five years after their accident, right after moving here. Neither of us was looking for a relationship, but it happened anyway. When his children found out about me, they quit speaking to him."

She grows silent, her lips pursed together, and her hands clenched tightly in her lap. Regardless of her efforts to control her emotions, tears escape her eyes and course down her cheeks.

"Margaret died two months before Harry. So many times, during the years that I loved him, I prayed for her death. Isn't that horrid? I wanted him not to have her so he could be all mine. I wanted him not to have to visit that horrid place anymore. He went every other weekend for twenty-five years. He took me once. Just to introduce us, he said. He never wanted me to go back, and I never did. I hurt for him. I cried so many tears over it. I wanted him to be free of her and the duty he had to her. It took me years to realize it wasn't duty that drove him there, it wasn't even guilt. It was love. Love is a steady and abiding thing, Olivia. Pain doesn't kill it. Mistakes don't kill it. I quit feeling anything for Marshall Elkins the day I found him with Corliss. In all the years that have passed, I have never stopped loving Harry Tyndale, just as he never stopped loving his Margaret. Maybe we are all given one certain person to love. Maybe we are only given one chance at real true love, and when we lose that, there's no way to escape the pain. What I've learned is that true love is worth whatever pain it brings. I know Daniel hurt you horribly. I know learning the truth about your birth doubled that pain. I can't blame you for being tempted to escape by any means possible, but I want you to make sure you aren't leaving love behind before leaping off any cliffs. That's all."

She stands up, and so do I. She hugs me tightly and leaves the room.

I wander through the patio doors to the pool. The night is warm, and the full moon blends with the pool's lights, tempting me with the pristine water that shimmers in the dark garden. I hesitate only a moment before slipping my dress over my head and sliding in with nothing on but my panties and bra.

Am I jumping off a cliff?

I close my eyes and lean back, spreading my arms out so I can float. Looking up at the moon, I drift on the water. It seems a million years ago that I met Daniel, but I still remember every detail of our first meeting, from what he was wearing to the smell of his cologne wafting toward me as I took his order.

I was surprised by the interest I saw in his dark eyes. I blushed and hurried away, but every time I looked his way, he was staring at me with the same expression.

The Friday after I first saw him, he came to the library, which was my favorite hangout. I was so surprised when he spoke to me that I dropped the book I was reading. He bent down and picked it up before I could get out of my chair.

He put it back in front of me, careful to leave it open to the page it had landed on. Botticelli's *Venus of Urbino* in all her nude glory filed one page, while Rubens' *Venus and Adonis* filled the other.

"What are you studying?"

"Nudes in art." I felt myself blush four shades of red and slammed the book shut. "I was just leaving."

He followed me down the row as I put the book back

in place on the shelf. "Do you have a test on it or something?"

"I'm doing my term paper on it. Why?"

"I was just wondering why you were here hiding out in the library on a Friday, looking at pictures of naked people. That seems kind of..."

"Pathetic?" I supplied when he paused to find the right word.

"That's your word, not mine," he said. Then he laughed. "Don't you have a boyfriend?"

I shook my head.

"I have friends who are boys, but none who are boyfriends." I knew I sounded like a geek.

"You want to go out and get some food?" he offered.

I hesitated only a minute. He wore a dark blue T-shirt that fit him like a second skin and a pair of jeans that set my heart pounding, and I couldn't refuse his invitation. He slipped on his jacket and grabbed my coat. Like the gentleman I would soon find out he was, he helped me on with it, and we left the library.

From then on, we were always together.

He asked me to marry him on Christmas Eve. He went to church with us, and as we slid into his car after the service, he turned to me.

"Marry me, Livy." He held out a velvet box with a small but beautiful marquis diamond resting inside. He told me later that he carried it around for three weeks waiting for the right moment to ask me.

****

Now, as I drift on the water, thinking of the day her daddy asked me to marry him, I feel the baby move for the first time. It's such a tiny little movement that, at first, I think I imagined it, but then I feel it again, and there is no mistaking it.

"I feel you," I breathe. "I feel you."

I run my hand over my belly, wanting to shout to everyone that the baby is moving, but there is no one to tell. Aunt Junie and Dianna are both in bed. Besides, they aren't the ones I want to tell anyway.

I hurry out of the pool and up the steps to my room. Once there, I dial our home number and listen to it ring. I am just about to hang up when I hear him growl a greeting into the phone.

"Did I wake you?"

"Livy?" he slurs, "Is that you?"

"Daniel, listen, there's something I need to tell you."

A sound that's halfway between a laugh and a sob echoes across the phone line.

"You don't have to tell me anything, babe. I was there. I saw you. I know what's happening, Olivia. I've just been waiting for the papers to arrive."

"What papers? What are you talking about?"

"The divorce papers. I'll sign them as soon as I get them."

"You want a divorce?" I feel as if the floor has dropped from beneath my feet.

His low curse is followed by the sound of breaking glass.

"Yes, I want a divorce, Livy," he cries. "That's just what I've been dreaming of. What the hell is taking you so long? You've made up your mind. Just send the damn papers!"

Another low curse and the line goes dead.

I hang the phone up without another word. Isn't this what I want? I ask myself. If so, why do I feel so bereft? And what does he mean he saw me?

I dial our number again, but I get a busy signal. I try his cell phone, but it goes straight to voicemail. Determined to get answers to my questions, I call Julie. If he's talked to anyone about wanting a divorce, it would be Earl.

"You've got to come home," Julie pleads. "You wouldn't even recognize him. He drinks constantly. He doesn't shave. He's doesn't go to work. He's been this way since he came to see you. He wouldn't tell us one damn thing except that you were happier there than here. Are you, Liv? Are you really happy?"

"I don't know what you're talking about. Daniel hasn't been here. I haven't heard from him in months. I assumed that meant he didn't want me to come home."

"Liv, honey, he calls you all the time. When he was still talking to us, he said there was no getting past Junie and Dianna. You were locked up tighter than Fort Knox."

"You mean he's called and they haven't let him talk to me?"

"They didn't tell you?"

"No. But still, Jules, he didn't come here."

"He came there, Livy. He drove down there and back in two days. He hasn't stopped drinking since he got home."

"Why didn't he talk to me?"

"That I don't know, hon. He won't answer the phone. He won't return our calls. He won't even answer the door. Earl went over to talk to him."

"Are you sure he's okay?" I can't keep the worry out of my voice.

"He's alive, if that's what you mean."

"How do you know?" I know he's alive, I just spoke

to him, but how can they be sure if they aren't checking? I need them to watch out for him.

"Earl and I called your parents when we couldn't get through to him. They were beginning to worry as well. They know where you hide the spare key, so they let themselves in."

"He wants a divorce," I told her.

"No, he doesn't."

"He told me he does."

"Well, he lied. You need to come home, Livy. Soon."

I don't make any promises before hanging up.

What is Daniel doing? How long will they hold his job if he's not going? He loves his job. Of course, he loves me, too, but that didn't stop him from risking losing me.

Apparently, my parents were the last people to see him, so they're the ones I need to talk to. Plus, Mama will be excited about me feeling the baby move.

Daddy answers, and as soon as I speak, Mama picks up the other extension. I can feel her disapproval through the line.

"Have you talked to Daniel?" I ask before she can say anything.

"Yes," Daddy said.

"Is he okay? Julie said he's drinking and hasn't been going to work."

"He's fine," Mama says crisply. "How are you and the baby?"

"Oh, Mama," I say, letting the wonder of it fill my voice. "I felt her move."

"Her?" she repeats. "Did the doctors say it was a girl? They can be wrong, you know, but they aren't wrong very often anymore."

"No, I haven't had my sonogram yet, but Opal says it's a girl."

"Opal?" Mama repeats, trying to sound confused.

"You know who Opal is, Mama."

"When are you coming home, Olivia?" Daddy asks, probably hoping he can diffuse Mama's explosion.

"Why in the world are you speaking to that woman?" Mama demands at the same time. "She doesn't even live there anymore. So you must have made a special trip to visit her."

Mama's voice has risen to that screeching whine that raises my hackles, and I want to snap right back at her, but I control myself. I didn't call to get in a screaming match with my mother. I called to make sure my husband is all right.

"Daddy, I just talked to Julie, and she told me about Daniel. I just want to make sure he's being taken care of."

"Does he know about the baby yet?" my mother barks.

"I don't know. He says he knows everything. So I assume he does."

"He's fine," she repeats her earlier mantra. "I went over yesterday and picked up a little and did his laundry. He's fine."

"Is he drinking?" Maybe we can remain calm enough to discuss this like adults.

"What does it matter, Olivia? You have a life far from here. At the moment, none of us or our lives here matter to you. The least you can do is make your break with Daniel swift and clean. The poor man has done everything he possibly can to get you to forgive him, but you continue to drag him along, not really saying you are coming home and not saying you aren't. Is this your punishment for us all, Olivia? We all hurt you, so now we're all just written out of your life? Maybe permanently, maybe just temporarily, but a little time in purgatory will serve us all right?"

"I'm not trying to punish anyone, Mama. I'm just trying to decide what is best for me and my child."

"Well, let us know when you decide, Olivia, because the way it is right now is sheer hell."

"I love you," I say, but the words seem empty when compared to the pain in my mother's voice.

"We love you, too, sweetheart," Daddy says.

"I miss you," I say, but they've already hung up.

Chapter Sixteen

"Has Daniel called me?" I'm sitting at the table eating orange marmalade on toast when Aunt Junie and Dianna come in from the patio the next morning.

Aunt Junie almost drops her coffee cup, and Dianna tries to slip back through the door to escape. My voice rises precariously. "Stop right there!"

The truth is written all over their guilt-ridden faces. They have purposely let me believe that Daniel hasn't even tried to contact me.

"How many times has he called?"

"A dozen," Junie says at the same moment Dianna says, "At least a hundred."

Junie shoots her a withering glance, and she shrugs.

"He called every damn day for weeks," Dianna says. "He's slacked up recently, though."

"Did he come here?"

"Where?"

"Don't you dare 'where' me! Here! Did he come to this city? This house? Did he come here to see me?"

"No!" they both say in mock horror, but I know they're lying.

"What did you do?" I cry. "What did you say to send him away?"

"Nothing," Junie says. "We just told him you weren't here. He went out looking for you. We assumed he didn't find you."

I rest my head in my hands as I absorb the fact that Daniel has been trying to reach me for months.

"Do you want to go home?" Dianna prods.

"God, yes," I say honestly. "But I want to go home months ago. I want to fix what went wrong before he has a chance to do what he did. I want to undo what happened. I don't know if I *can* go home now. Even if I wanted to."

"Maybe you should call him, talk to him."

"I did," I admit miserably. "I called last night. He told me he's been waiting for the divorce papers. He said he wants a divorce."

"Damn it," Aunt Junie swears. "That man needs to get his head out of his ass and figure out what he wants."

"That's basically what I told him," Dianna says. "I probably should have just kept my mouth shut."

The baby moves, and I run my hand across my belly soothingly. It seems we both agree with Dianna.

Chapter Seventeen

Daniel

No matter how much I drink, I can't wash away
Olivia's face. Her laughter, the sound that so intrigued
me the first time I met her, now drives me to the edge of
sanity.

I've been drunk for days, weeks, months. I have no
real idea how much time has passed. I quit going to work,
and I can't make myself care if they hold my job or give
it to someone who's actually there. What does it matter
how many new buildings get built or how many old ones
are demolished when my house is as cold and silent as a
tomb?

Olivia has always taken care of the bills, so the first
month she was gone, I never even thought about it. The
second month, the incessant ringing of the telephone and
the subsequent spiel by bill collectors reminded me they
needed to be taken care of. When I came back from
Junie's, I decided I really didn't give a damn about any
of it. I ripped the phone cords out of the wall and set
about drowning myself in liquor.

Sylvia and Oliver come by and check on me every
few days. Sylvia clucks around washing clothes and
dishes and making sure I have enough food in the house,
as if I eat anymore. Oliver sits silently staring at me,
nursing a scotch as I guzzle whatever open bottle is

handy.

The day they find me sitting in the dark because the lights are shut off for nonpayment, Sylvia is livid.

"You're killing yourself, Daniel," she scolds, throwing the window open to let in at least a hint of air.

"I don't care, Sylvia."

"Don't say that!" she cries. "Olivia needs you. The—"

Oliver clears his throat, and she stops, turning away with a cry of dismay.

I don't even bother to argue with her or wonder what she was about to say. I just roll to my side so my back is facing her and pretend I'm asleep until she's gone.

Before she leaves, she asks me if she can start paying the bills. She doesn't want me to live without electricity, but I demand she leave my life in my own hands. She throws the mail at me and storms out without another word. Obviously, she takes the light bill with her, because a few hours later, I'm blinded by the overhead light and the air conditioner kicks in.

A few hours later, the phone rings.

"Great," I groan as I stand up and stagger toward it. As my eyes focus, I see the recently replaced phone jack and line. Apparently, my father-in-law decided I need to have the phone ringing at all hours of the day and night. I'm tempted to rip it out again, but something makes me answer.

I'm so surprised to hear Olivia's voice through the phone that I'm speechless. A small but surprising bit of hope surges through me. Maybe she's coming home.

"Listen, I need to tell you something," she says, and reality crashes down on me.

I make some sort of sound—I don't even know what

it is, a laugh or a sob. It is all I can do not to beg her to come home. Tears choke me as I tell her I saw her, and she doesn't need to tell me anything. I'm just waiting for the papers to come.

"What papers? What are you talking about?" Her confusion is so genuine, I'm tempted to applaud her. My little wife has become quite the actress. She must have taken lessons from her crazy aunt.

"The divorce papers. I'll sign them as soon as I get them."

"You want a divorce?" She deserves more than applause for the heartbreak in her voice. She deserves an Oscar.

I throw my whiskey glass across the room, and it shatters into a million pieces.

I say something about wanting a divorce, not even sure what I'm saying, not caring if I hurt her. I yank the phone cords from the wall again and throw the phone across the room.

In the silence that follows, anger turns back to pain.

Chapter Eighteen

Olivia

When I call my parents' house a week later, Mama answers on the second ring. Her voice sounds old and weary.

"Hi, Mama, it's me? Are you okay?"

"I'm fine, Olivia. How are you?" I can tell she's still put out, by the frostiness in her tone, so I decide to jump right into why I'm calling.

"I'm fine. My sonogram is scheduled for next week, and I was wondering if you and Daddy want to come down and go with me."

The ice thaws as she agrees, but like always, she has to ask one more question. I can remember so many times when we could have avoided an argument without that one more question she invariably asks. I wonder why she hasn't learned by now.

"Have you called Daniel? He could ride with us, help your daddy drive down."

"No, I haven't called Daniel, and I don't intend to."

"Olivia," she begins, but breaks off quickly. Perhaps she is finally learning. "We'll see you Monday night."

****

By the day of the sonogram, I'm so nervous I can barely function. I am truly trying to believe the baby is fine, but I want proof. Of course, even then, my worries won't end, but for a little while, my hope will be restored.

When it's time to leave, I follow Mama and Daddy to the car. Aunt Junie is still in the house, so we wait for her. As I slip into the car, Mama turns to me.

"Why is she coming?" she snaps.

"I asked her to."

"If you were going to ask her, you could have left me and your father alone. We came down so you wouldn't have to face this alone."

I'm stung by her words and her tone.

"I'm sorry to have bothered you, Mama. If you'd rather not go, I can just have Aunt Junie drive me, and you and Daddy can go on home."

"Sylvia, calm down," my father says, trying to soothe her ruffled feathers. "It isn't the end of the world that Junie's going. I'm sure Olivia didn't mean to upset you. Besides, I've always wanted to see one of these things. People are always flapping those pictures around, and I can't make out a darn thing. Maybe if I see a moving picture, I'll be able to tell what I'm looking at."

Leave it to Daddy to make a trip to the obstetrician sound like a great learning experience while at the same time heading trouble between Mama and me off at the pass.

"I suppose you're right. It just seems unfair that all three of us are going to see the baby, and Daniel doesn't even know he or she exists."

"Mother," I groan in exasperation.

"I'm just going to sit here and be quiet," she vows. "Obviously, no one cares to hear my opinion."

I'm somehow able to keep my mouth shut and not let loose a hallelujah.

****

111

The ultrasound technician talks nonstop as she covers my belly in warm goo and runs the wand over the mound that houses my child.

Mama, Daddy, and Aunt Junie all watch in fascination as she points out hands and feet, legs, and arms. They gasp at evidence of her tiny beating heart, and then again when the baby's face turns toward us.

"Do you want to know the sex?" the technician asks.

"Yes," we all answer at once.

The technician smiles and moves the wand once more.

"It's a girl," she announces. "And everything about her appears to be perfect."

Tears of relief prick my eyes. She's fine, she's perfect and healthy. And I will do everything in my power to keep her that way.

Until now, I haven't realized how much I want it to be a girl. I'm not sure why, but a few reasons pop into my head and none of them are pleasant. A girl will be easier to raise without a father. A boy feels too much like I'm trying to make up for my loss. I push all the reasons away and force myself to give in to my parents' joy.

"We have to go shopping," Mama exclaims. "I'm dying to buy something lacy and pink."

Aunt Junie seconds the idea, and Daddy has no choice but to go along with them.

****

I take my parents to see the gallery the next day. Neither of them is enthusiastic about going, but they agree to come along anyway.

I have already shown them the entire building, and we are standing in the downstairs studio when Peter walks in.

His face brightens when he sees us.

"Olivia!" he says coming toward me with a brilliant smile. "I wasn't expecting you to be here today."

He opens his arms, intending I'm sure to hug me, but I turn toward my parents.

"Peter, I'd like you to meet my parents. Oliver and Sylvia Darlington. Mama, Daddy, this is Peter Salazar. He owns the gallery. I'll be running it for him."

"I thought you were leasing it, and running it for yourself," Mama says, ignoring Peter completely as Daddy shakes his hand.

"The gallery was my late wife's, and I've decided I simply can't let it go. Olivia has graciously agreed to let me hire her to make it the perfect legacy for Paulina."

My mother sizes him up with one long, all-encompassing glance. "And the two of you will be working together?"

"For a while, yes. We'll work together very closely to make sure the re-opening goes smoothly. After that, I have the utmost faith that Olivia will do fine with only the minimum contact between us. If that's how she wants it."

He is looking at me instead of my mother, and I wonder if the desire that smolders in the sapphire depth of his eyes is palpable to my parents. I wonder if they can see how close I've been to giving in to his unspoken invitation. I quickly turn the conversation to something else.

"I had the sonogram," I say. "It really is a girl."

Before I know what he's going to do, he reaches out to caress my stomach.

"So, Opal was right, eh?" He chuckles. "It really will be a beautiful baby girl, with her mother's smile."

My father clears his throat, and I turn to them.

"I think it's time we head back to Junie's." It is one of the few times in my life I can remember my father's voice being tinged with disapproval.

My mother, on the other hand, remains totally silent.

I'm on edge as we drive back to Junie's in silence. By the time we all sit down to supper, I'm jumpy as a cat.

"These shrimp are delicious, Dianna," Mama says, popping one into her mouth.

"I'm glad you're enjoying them." Dianna, like me, is watching her warily, as if waiting for the outburst.

"What did you think of the studio?" Junie asks, and I wish I could give her a quick kick under the table.

"It's very beautiful," Mama says. "We met the owner. He seems like a nice gentleman. Doesn't he, Oliver?"

"I didn't care for him much," my father says. "A little too debonair for my tastes."

He looks at me pointedly, and I feel heat rise to my face.

Surprisingly, it is my mother who turns the conversation to something else. I am thankful for the reprieve, but I know it is just that.

I'm already in bed when she knocks softly on my door. Without waiting for an answer, she comes inside and perches on the side of my bed. The moonlight through the sheer curtains softens her features and blurs the telltale signs of age so that she looks young again, like the mother of my childhood. From reading me bedtime stories to talks about the birds and the bees, she perched there on the side of my bed night after night. It was the time of day her busyness finally ceased, she set her worries aside, and she gave me her full attention. Tonight, she seems a million miles away.

"Is everything okay, Mama?"

She looks at me, and in the pale light, I can see the glimmer of tears in her eyes. My own eyes fill in response.

"You know it isn't, Olivia." Her voice is soft and holds none of the anger or disapproval that has been there recently. She runs her hand over mine, perhaps readying herself for what she'll say next. "I want you to be careful. You know I love you, and I love Daniel, too. He's been a part of you and a part of our family for so long that I can't help but think of him as a son. I'm sorry if my pushing you back to him hurts and angers you, but it's difficult for me to see you alone. I know it isn't as uncommon or frowned upon for a woman to be alone now as it used to be, but a heart alone is still as sad as it ever was."

"I don't know what to do," I admit as a tear rolls down my cheek. "I still love Daniel, but I don't know if I can forgive him yet. I don't know if I ever can."

"And you don't have to decide that right now. Forgiveness takes time. Even once you say you'll forgive him, it's going to be a constant battle to actually do it. If we could forget, forgiveness would be much easier, but God didn't wire us that way. Our biggest mistakes live on in infamy, haunting us and those we hurt for the rest of our lives."

She looks away, and I think maybe she's remembering a hurt of her own. As I did the day I found out about Daniel, I suspect she has known betrayal, but I don't want to hear about my father's infidelity or hers. Finally, she shakes her head and offers me a wistful smile.

"Peter is a very handsome man. Very charismatic. And obviously very attracted to you. His gallery is lovely, and I know having a gallery is something you've always wanted. But I want you to consider what you're doing very carefully. I'm not going to try to talk you out of it. I'm your mother. I want you to be happy. But I don't want you to do something that will cause you unhappiness or make it impossible for you to return to reality when this illusion ends."

"What illusion?" My hackles are beginning to rise, and Mama makes a soft soothing sound as she smooths the quilt.

"You know what illusion, Olivia. Peter is not your husband, and you have no business taking a lover until you're divorced. You can't continue to wander around Key West pretending there aren't loose ends in your life that need to be tied up. The gallery is an illusion, sweetheart. It looks like it's yours, but Peter will always be there, the one who really owns it. He's the one who will pull the strings, and to keep up the illusion, you'll have to dance to his tune. And you may not like the one he chooses."

I make a soft sound of protest, but she keeps talking.

"Olivia, I saw the way the two of you looked at each other. You're playing with fire. I just don't want to see you get burned." She kisses me on the forehead, and for just a moment, I'm her little girl again, and I'm alone and frightened. My arms wrap around her, and I cling to her for a few precious seconds. She kisses me once more before standing. "Good night, sweetheart. I know you'll make the right decisions. I'm not telling you what they are, but you need to hurry up and make them before it's too late."

****

I'm surprised when Mama doesn't try to lecture me before heading to their car the next morning. Somehow, she and I have come to an unspoken truce. Still, I feel a little lost when she and Daddy load their bags into the trunk without another word about me coming home.

"I love you, Mama," I say, leaning into the passenger side window.

She smiles at me and puts a hand on my cheek. Her voice is sweet but certain. "I love you, too, Olivia. And I'll see you soon."

Chapter Nineteen

Daniel

"Get up, Daniel! Get up this minute."

I crack my eyes open and find Sylvia standing beside the couch with the vacuum. Her hair is covered with a bandana and an apron is tied around her waist. Elbow-length green rubber gloves are the finishing touch to her costume.

"What in the hell are you doing?" I moan and cover my face with my arm.

"I'm saving you from yourself. Get up and get dressed. Shave, take a bath, put on clean clothes. I've done my best to keep this place livable, but it is time for a real cleaning. When my daughter comes home, I do not want her to come home to this pigsty." She waves her arms around to encompass the whole room, possibly the whole house.

"Sylvia, Livy's not coming home. For God's sake, she's gone into business down there. She's in love."

She puts her hands on her hips and looks at me as if I've lost my mind.

"She's in love with you, just as she's always been."

"I saw her. She's in love with the man who owns that damn art gallery. She was *glowing.* I've never seen her look so beautiful. Or so happy. I won't ruin that for her. I love her too much not to want to see her happy."

"Bull," she says and flips on the vacuum.

My head is pounding, and in an effort to escape the noise, I go to the bathroom. For the first time in weeks, I look in the mirror. I've grown a full beard and my hair needs more than a trim. I don't really care what I look like, since I'm only taking a shower to drown out the noise of the vacuum. Still, I trim up the beard before stepping into the shower. The water pounds over my head, and I lift my face, letting it wash away some of the lingering effects of the alcohol. After I'm done with the shower, I run the tub full of water and have a good soak, and then I shower again.

When I'm dressed in clean clothes, I come through the bedroom door. The living room and kitchen are immaculate. Sylvia has rearranged the couch and television so that it faces the open veranda doors. The whole house smells like lemon and oil soap. She's standing there on the patio, her arms folded over her chest, surveying the room from the outside.

"You shouldn't have moved the furniture by yourself," I say. "I would have helped."

"I'm fine. They're both on rollers, so it wasn't that difficult."

"It looks and smells great in here. Thank you."

"You look better, too." She comes back inside. "You smell quite a bit better too."

I shrug and grunt out a thank you.

"Sit down," she orders, and I sit on the couch while she remains standing. "There are some things I need to tell you."

I don't know what to expect from her. I've never seen her the way she is now, subdued and almost ashamed.

"On the day Olivia walked in on you and that woman, she came to our house. She wanted comfort, rest, a safe haven to sort things out. I don't know why we couldn't just give her that."

She throws her hands up in the air in frustration and begins to pace.

"We should have just given her a bed and a shoulder to cry on. Instead, we chose that time, *that very moment*, to unburden a secret we've carried all her life. I'm not even sure why we thought it was a good idea. It seemed like the right time when we started. But by the time we were done, we realized it wasn't. She was too hurt, too vulnerable. It must have seemed as if everything steady in her life crashed down around her ears in one single day."

"What was it?" What could they have possibly told her that would not have been dwarfed by what she saw in my office?

"We adopted Olivia. Junetta gave birth to her. We wanted a baby so badly, and when Junetta got pregnant and couldn't keep the baby, it seemed logical that we take her. It just never seemed necessary to tell Olivia. We thought about it through the years, but we told ourselves it wasn't important, that it didn't matter in the long run. I don't know why we pretended she wouldn't care. Looking back, I think I was just afraid for her to find out. She was always so fascinated by Junetta. The way she lived, those people who lived with her. I was afraid that if I told her Junetta was her mother, she would want to be with her because she was more exciting, more beautiful, more everything than I was."

I massage my temples. The hangover I've avoided with constant alcohol consumption for the last few weeks is coming on with a vengeance.

"You told her all this *that* day?"

She nods her head and begins to cry.

"She was furious. I think she was just as hurt by our breach of trust as she was by yours. That's why she went to Junetta's. That's why she stays."

"Jesus, Sylvia, how could you have done that to her? No wonder she won't come home!" I don't mean to yell, but I can't help it. Anger has replaced everything else I've known.

"Don't you think Oliver and I know how wrong we were? My God, Daniel, she hates us! I want her home," her voice softens to a whisper. "I just want her home."

She leans against the patio door, and it takes me a minute or so to realize something is wrong.

"Sylvia?" I yell her name as she turns to me, her face a mottled gray. I reach her just as she makes a small mewling sound and collapses.

****

I sit with Oliver in the hospital waiting room, praying the doctor will come out soon. We know only that Sylvia has suffered a heart attack, but we can only wait to find out how badly it damaged her.

Oliver buries his face in his hands, and quiet sobs shake his shoulders. I place a hand on his back, hoping it will offer some measure of comfort.

"This is just how her mother went," he says. "She was fine, laughing, talking, playing with Olivia. Then, *bam*. Just like that, she was just gone. No good-byes, nothing. It nearly killed Sylvia to lose her that way."

"We aren't going to lose Sylvia," I assure him, but I know my assurances are meaningless.

"We've got to tell Olivia. She should be here."

"I'll call her as soon as we've spoken to the doctor. She's going to demand a lot of answers, and I need to have as many as possible before I call her."

Thirty minutes later, a grim-faced doctor comes through the doors. I try to make eye contact, but his gaze evades me every time our eyes meet. I know his news is not going to be good.

"Mr. Darlington," he says, shaking Oliver's hand and then mine. "Your wife has suffered a massive heart attack. There's little likelihood of recovery. I don't expect she'll regain consciousness. I'm sorry."

Oliver sways where he stands, and I gently push him back into the chair.

"Thank you," I say as I shake the doctor's hand again.

"Your wife should get here as quickly as possible."

Chapter Twenty

Olivia

The flight home seems endless. When I'm not praying for my mother to recover, I'm worrying about how Daniel will react when he sees me. I'm obviously pregnant now, and even if I wanted to, I can't hide it any longer.

At the hospital, I find my mother's room. Amid the myriad wires and tubes connected to her and the bed, she looks even tinier than usual. Perhaps it's because she's so quiet and still. It feels as if she's disappearing, a small fading shadow of herself.

"Hi, Mama." I kiss her cheek, but she doesn't move, doesn't respond at all. I know the doctors say she won't survive, that we have only hours with her, at the most, but in my heart, I can't help hoping and praying they're wrong.

"Olivia," my father says from his place in the corner. He too has become smaller, his shoulders hunched and his face pale and drawn. He stands, and I rush into his arms. We hold each other as we cry, both knowing our lives won't be the same without her.

"Has anything changed?" I ask, hoping to hear better news than what he gave me over the phone.

"No," he says, his eyes going lovingly to my mother. "She's still here."

His unspoken acceptance that the only change in my mother's condition will be her dying speaks volumes.

He looks back at me, touches my stomach tenderly, then my face. "Ah, Livy, how beautiful you are."

Tears fill my eyes as he goes to my mother and bends close to her ear.

"Olivia's here, sweetheart. Even more beautiful than she was the last time we saw her. Looks like the baby's growing like she should be."

He straightens and motions to the chair behind me. "Sit."

"How did it happen?" I ask as I lower my somewhat bulky frame into the chair. I pull the blanket that is already there around me, trying to ward off the chill that has settled over me.

"Daniel's been having a rough time of it. She's been going by every few days, but they had quite a row last time she was over, so she hasn't been in a while. He won't answer the phone. She worries about him. She's afraid he's going to drink himself to death. Yesterday morning, she woke up in a snit. She said she'd had enough of this foolishness, that she was going to get him off that couch and she was going to get the house ready for your return. Neither Daniel nor I have been able to convince her you're not coming back."

"Was she there when it happened?"

He nodded. "Apparently, she finally got him off the couch, cleaned the house, told him about Junetta, and collapsed. He's been here with me ever since."

"Where is he now?"

"I convinced him to go for a walk. He should be back any minute. Does he know about the baby yet?"

"No."

"Olivia, what in the world are you thinking?"

"I don't know, Dad," I say honestly. "I just couldn't tell him the day I found out about his affair, not after walking in on him like that, and there hasn't been a good time since then."

He looks at me sternly just as the door opens and a man walks in carrying two Styrofoam cups.

He has a beard, his cheeks are hollow, and his clothes hang off his frame. Head bowed, he moves slowly, as if uncertain his legs will both hold him and propel him along. It takes me a minute or two to recognize him as my husband.

"Daniel?" I'm surprised and dismayed by his appearance.

He lifts bloodshot eyes to my face.

"Olivia," he sighs my name, as if a great weight has been lifted from his shoulders. "You came."

"Of course I came." The pain in his eyes, the weariness of his body, erase everything else, and I want nothing more than to wrap my arms around him and have his wrapped around me. For the moment, I forget the pain that swirls around us and the secret I still carry.

I surge to my feet, the blanket slipping to the floor as I do. A guttural curse escapes him.

"Daniel," I speak his name, reaching for him, wanting to blunt the shock, wipe the anguish from his face, but he steps back.

"You're pregnant."

"It's a girl."

His mouth and throat work spastically as he moves past me to hand a cup of coffee to my father. He sets the other on the windowsill.

Without a word to my father or me, he walks out of

the room.

I stand there dumbfounded, staring at the door. I knew he would be angry, but I never thought he would simply walk away. The baby gives an energetic kick, as if spurring me into action, and I rush from the room.

The hallway between the room and the elevators is empty except for two nurses waiting for the elevator. He couldn't have already gone down. I head toward the bank of windows at the other end of the hall. Outside, the city lights are bright against the night sky, but I barely spare them a glance as I turn into the corridor to my left. Daniel is there, his arms pressed against the wall, his face buried against them. Even from here, I can see his shoulders heaving. Without thinking of how we got to this point, I rush to him and wrap my arms around his waist.

He turns toward me, bringing me against him, and finally, I am in his arms, held firmly against a chest that feels so familiar yet so foreign. He has been changed by our ordeal, just as I have, and I know neither of us is likely to be the same. He holds me for only a moment, before he drops his arms and steps back.

I run a hand over my belly, and he watches, something akin to horror replacing the pain in his eyes. Was I wrong to think he would be happy about the baby? My hand stops moving, as if protecting her from her father's cold reception to her existence.

"Are you still seeing Melanie?" I blurt out. We should both remember who was in the wrong here.

"What?" he looks at me in confusion. "No."

I step to the window, looking out over the serenity gardens below.

"Does it matter?" he demands. "If I'm seeing Melanie or not?"

"Of course it matters," I snap. "Why wouldn't it?"

"If we're divorcing, I don't see how it could possibly matter to you who I see."

"Divorcing?" I repeat the word, horrified that he is still saying it.

"Don't tell me you've changed your mind. Not now." He waves a hand toward my belly, and his voice trails off.

Shock and hurt bring tears to my eyes, and I fight to keep them at bay. How had I almost let my mother convince me he wanted me home?

"I guess your parents knew. They went down a few weeks ago, didn't they?"

I nod. "They came for the sonogram."

"Did they?" his voice is ice, his eyes fire. "Did they meet him then?"

"Who?"

"Your lover."

"What?"

A sharp bark of bitter laughter escapes him, and I recognize his sense of betrayal for what it is. I suddenly remember Junie and Dianna's guilt when I asked them if he'd been there.

"I came to Key West, Liv," he confirms. "I went to that gallery you're opening. You weren't there, so I figured you were down at Mallory Square. I know you love watching the sunset there. And I was right. There you were. Coming out of a hotel, with *him*. I saw the way he looked at you, the way he touched you." His voice breaks, and he slams a hand on the wall. "My God, Olivia, you were so beautiful. Glowing. And now you're…"

He didn't finish the sentence.

"Oh my God, Daniel, no." I put my hand on his arm, part of me thinking he deserves the misery he's in, while the rest of me wants only to stop his pain. "Peter isn't my lover. And the baby isn't his. She's yours. I was pregnant when I came to your office that day. That's *why* I was there."

"You've been pregnant the whole time you were gone?" Anger sharpens his voice. "Why didn't you tell me?"

A brittle laugh escapes me. "I tried. You were a little preoccupied."

"It's been six months, Liv. You've had plenty of time to tell me before now."

He was right, of course, but I was so angry at his accusations I couldn't admit it.

"Like you could have told me about Melanie? Or my parents could have told me about Junie? I don't think any of you needs to lecture me on being honest and forthright."

"So this was your payback? You were going to have my baby and raise it without me? And if you were lucky, I'd never find out? Is that what you thought?"

"Not really, no. To be honest, I wasn't sure you'd care."

Silence reigns for interminable seconds before he gives a shuddering sigh and runs his hand over my hair.

"Ah, Livy," he says sadly. "It really is over, isn't it?"

Chapter Twenty-One

Daniel

The shock of seeing Olivia so obviously pregnant is the biggest surprise of my life. I know Olivia. I know she didn't have sex with someone days after she left me. I know she's too far along for anyone but me to be the father. But the hurt I feel is so deep, I can't get past the idea that another man is the only reason she would have kept such a secret. Knowing I deserve it doesn't make it any less painful.

I barely make it out of Sylvia's hospital room before being overtaken by my emotions. When I was ten, I lost both my parents in a plane crash. When I was nineteen, the aunt who raised me, after their death, passed away in her sleep. I was so hurt and alone, but Olivia and her family took me in and loved me. Her parents have been like parents to me for all the years we've been together, and they have treated me like a son since the first time I came through their door with Olivia. And now I'm losing them. Sylvia is dying, and Oliver will never be the same.

It's obvious I've lost Olivia. After what I did, it's not surprising, but even the slight hope that she will forgive me and come home has been all I've had. Now that hope is completely gone. I lean my head against the wall. I have hit rock bottom, and I am well and truly alone in my grief.

"Daniel." Her arms come wrapping around me from behind. A sob rattles from my lungs as I turn to face her. It feels so right to have her there against my chest, even with the barrier of her child between us. I hold her for as long as I can before I step back, knowing there are things we have to say.

We stare at each other for a long moment, wondering where to start. Her eyes are deep blue pools, the tears illuminated by the harsh glare of the hospital lights. She licks her lips nervously, and one of her hands moves to caress her burgeoning belly. Memories hit me like hail, as I remember feeling our son move beneath my touch. It was months after she first felt him that I finally did. Has she already felt this one? Does she lie in bed, as she did then, running a hand over her belly, talking to the baby, singing those silly songs she remembers from childhood? And then, in horror, I imagine *him* there with her, his long tan fingers splayed over her white skin, feeling my child dance within her.

Her hand stops moving.

"Are you still seeing Melanie?" she demands.

I've forgotten all about Melanie, and for a minute, I'm thrown by the question.

"What? No."

She says nothing as she turns to the window. Anger at her dismissiveness surges through me.

I demand to know why she cares if she's divorcing me, and then when she feigns confusion, I am all the angrier.

"Don't tell me you've changed your mind. Not now." I wave a hand toward her, encompassing the baby and all it entails. Why had Sylvia told me she wanted to come home when it was so obvious she didn't?

She tells me her parents came down for the sonogram. *My* child's sonogram, the child I'd known nothing about.

"Did they? Did they meet him then?"

"Who?"

"Your lover." I regret them the moment the words leap from my mouth, an accusation I wish I could recall. But it's too late. She looks at me as if I'm dirt, as if I deserve the sin of omission she has committed, that she would still be committing if she hadn't been forced to return by her mother's illness.

"What?" Her voice is calm and cold, while my own is a wild, ragged tangle of pain as I admit that I came to Key West, that I saw her there with him, that I *know.*

"Daniel, no," she says, placing a hand on my arm. I stare at that familiar hand, the light veins beneath her skin, the neatly manicured nails, painted a Sylvia-approved light pink. I listen to her soft voice insist that the man, Peter, isn't her lover, that the baby is mine. That she found out she was pregnant the morning she came to my office. That's why she was there. I hear myself ask her why she hadn't told me, and her ugly bark of laughter. All this time, she knew I wasn't with Melanie. Julie would have told her that, but she didn't tell me she was pregnant.

"It's been six months. You could have told me before now."

"Like you could have told me about Melanie? Or my parents could have told me about Junie? I don't think anyone needs to lecture me on being honest and forthright."

"So this was your payback? You were going to have my baby and raise it without me? And if you were lucky,

I'd never find out? Is that what you thought?"

"Not really, no. To be honest, I wasn't sure you'd care."

Her words, spoken so softly, without anger, without anything but truth tingeing them, nearly brings me to my knees. If after all the years we've loved each other, all the days and nights we've spent dreaming of a child, she can look me in the eye and say such a thing, I know our life together is over. Whatever hope there might be for us is so entangled in mistakes and punishment, lies and half-truths, omissions and accusations, it is totally useless.

I touch her face, just one last caress, before I leave. As I walk away from her, I know it's over. If she doesn't have the strength to file for divorce, I'll find an attorney and file for one tomorrow. It may seem like horrible timing, but it's best to get the ball rolling while she's here. Then she can go back to the Keys, where she's decided she belongs.

Chapter Twenty-Two

Olivia

After Daniel leaves, I go back to my mother's room to sit vigil with my father. Death is coming, and we both know there's no way to stop it. All we can do is pray it will be an easy and peaceful passage.

Daddy talks to her almost continuously, sometimes aloud, of memories and times the three of us shared, and sometimes at her ear, words shared by the two of them alone. I occasionally step out to give him moments alone with her and their memories together. At ten o'clock, he stands to his feet.

"I'm going to get a cup of coffee," he says. "Can I bring you anything?"

"Do you want me to go?" I ask. "I know you don't like leaving her."

"No, I think she'll be fine." He lays his hand on my hair. "Why don't you talk to her a bit. She'd like that."

I move my chair closer to her bedside and take her hand. I cannot think of the woman lying there as anything other than what she's always been: my mother. I know the change between us is only in my own head, caused by the things I now know. In my heart, however, there has been no change. She is still the woman who tucked me into bed every night, who read me stories, and who soothed my fears. She is the woman who both forced and coaxed me into the woman I am. Like a gardener, it was my mother who clipped and snipped stray limbs and wild shoots, training me to climb and grow and bloom as I was meant to do.

I run my fingers over the delicate skin on the back of her hand. Despite all the changes the rest of her body has seen over the years, her hands are still remarkably the same as they were when I was a little girl. I remember sitting in church, holding her hand, playing with her rings, and tracing the lines of her hands.

I can still see those hands wiping bright blue polish off my nails and pressing tissues into my own hands at all the appropriate moments. She still helps me take off my fingernail polish because I rarely remember to buy remover. When I show up at her house with chipped polish, she always notices and removes it immediately. Then she files and repaints them, rarely asking my opinion of whatever color she chooses.

While I am sadly lacking in purse-packing skills, Mama carries all necessary equipment in her ever-present handbag. If I'm lucky, I can sometimes find a restaurant napkin in my purse when I need one, but never a tissue. Headache, heartburn, blisters from wearing the wrong shoes—my mother always has the remedy there. If a game asking what's in your purse is played at showers for expectant mothers and brides-to-be, my mother is the person to beat. From safety pins to staple removers, she has it all and more in her purse. What is more amazing to me, she never has to dig around for it. She simply reaches in and pulls out whatever she's looking for, while I spend an inordinate amount of time digging around in the abyss for my car keys.

As I sit here, waiting for her to leave us, I wonder

with increasing dread how I'll survive without her.

With a sob, I turn her hand over and study the lines in her palm as if I can tell what the future holds, as if I can possibly change it.

I see nothing, of course, and I lift her hand and place a kiss on her palm.

"I'm so sorry, Mama," I say. I don't elaborate. If she can hear me, she is welcome to assign my apology to any number of transgressions. I'd prefer if she let it cover them all. "I don't want you to go."

I place her hand on my stomach, as the baby kicks.

"That's your granddaughter. Remember when I was pregnant with Danny? He always kicked when you touched my stomach. You felt him more than Daniel did." My voice breaks, but I force myself to continue. "When you see him in heaven, tell him I love him."

Daddy is leaning near her, whispering something only she can hear when Mama takes her last breath a few hours later. In the dark silence that follows, I hear Daddy's deep voice whispering good-bye.

Chapter Twenty-Three

Daniel

I go straight home from the hospital and take up my place on the sofa. I gulp whiskey from the one bottle Sylvia managed to miss when she was cleaning, but I realize quickly enough that it isn't what I want, so I dig in the medicine cabinet for a bottle of sleep aid I know Olivia keeps there. I take two, washing them down with water instead of the whiskey I'm tempted to use, and I lie back down on the couch.

It's nearly dawn when I hear the key turn in the lock and open my eyes to find Olivia standing over me. I am instantly awake and on my feet, knowing without being told why she is here.

"She's gone," she wails and falls against me.

We sit on the couch for a long time as I hold her. At some point, her sobs quiet, and I realize she's fallen asleep. I gently rouse her enough to lead her to the bedroom, where I help her undress and watch her slide into bed. I am turning away when she reaches out to me.

"Don't leave me," she says, and I can't deny her request.

I climb in beside her and wrap her in my arms. I savor the feel of her here in our bed where she belongs, and I vow to be there for her for the next few days. I can't leave her alone to face the loss of her mother. That is as far into the future as I dare to look.

Chapter Twenty-Four

Olivia

We bury Mama three days later, right beside Danny's grave. There under the swaying branches of the oak tree, we stand together, Daddy, Daniel, and I. Aunt Junie and Dianna stand behind me, Junie crying as if she's lost her best friend. Although I try to convince myself it is just proof of her acting ability, I am prone to believe her grief is real. Regardless of the differences she and Mama had, they had a bond that could never be broken despite the wedge it drove between them.

There are others here, Julie and Earl, men and women who have known my parents for years, people from church, and ladies from Mama's book club. I try to meet every gaze to convey my appreciation for their attendance and support.

I feel Peter's eyes on me before I see him standing behind everyone else, and a gasp escapes me. Daniel looks at me questioningly. Then his eyes follow mine. He stiffens, anger wafting from him as he faces the man he's not yet convinced isn't my lover. I have no idea how Peter came to be here at my mother's funeral, but I know without question his presence is an enormous mistake.

The preacher reads a passage of scripture, and one of the ladies from church steps forward to sing the hymn Daddy requested. Finally, it is time for us to bid our final farewell so the casket can be lowered into the ground. I walk to the casket, and Daniel is close behind me. I run my hand over the smooth glossy wood and lay my head against it. It is cold against my burning forehead and eyes.

"I love you, Mama," I whisper. "Watch over my baby."

Daniel, places one hand on my back, and presses the other against the coffin. I can feel his trembling, and I bite my lip to keep back a sob. I cover his hand with mine and lift my gaze to his. He offers me a watery smile and kisses my forehead. He will miss her nearly as much as I will.

As we walk away, I wonder how I can bear to have both Mama and Danny here now, how I will find the strength to visit them in this silent sanctuary of death. I look back at my father, still standing beside Mama's coffin. One day, sooner rather than later, he will be here, too.

The thought is too much for me. The ground wavers, and my knees buckle beneath me.

"Liv!" Daniel catches me before I fall.

Around us, people gasp, and voice their concern.

"Is she all right, Daniel?" one of Mama's book club ladies calls, hurrying toward us.

"I'm okay," I answer as Daniel brings me snug against his side and moves toward the car.

"You've got to take care of yourself, Olivia," the woman says, patting me on the arm. "Your Mama wouldn't want you to be upset."

I wonder if she knows how often my emotions went against what my mama wanted. I can almost hear Mama's admonitions now.

"Let us know if you and your daddy need anything, Liv," someone else says as we pass.

"Sylvia was a good woman. I know she's in a better place."

"I'm so glad you and your daddy still have each other."

The platitudes follow us across the cemetery.

"Olivia." Peter's voice reaches me just as Daniel opens the car door. I turn toward him, meeting his worried gaze. He embraces me, and I hope it looks like nothing more than a friendly gesture of condolence. He steps back, his arms sliding down my arms to take my hands in his. "I called your aunt's house looking for you, and she told me about your mother. I'm so sorry. I didn't want you to face this alone."

"She isn't alone," Daniel snaps.

"Of course not," Peter answers graciously, still holding my hands, "but I wanted to be sure she was being taken care of."

The tension between them is so thick it's palpable. I pray they don't make a scene.

Aunt Junie and Dianna are coming toward us, with Daddy shuffling between them. I pull my hands away from Peter and rush toward them, leaving Daniel and Peter to their own devices.

"C'mon, Daddy," I say. "We've got to go home."

"It won't be home without her," he says, and I know he's right. It will never feel like home again.

People come and go at the house all day. Mama's friends have more food spread out than we will ever eat, and when I open the refrigerator, I realize there's even more there.

I make my rounds, greeting people, thanking them

for coming, and keeping my eye on my father. He's being bombarded by people sharing their condolences and memories of Mama, and I am afraid he's going to collapse under the weight of his grief and his exhaustion at any minute.

Julie and Dianna are godsends, winding things up and kindly but efficiently guiding people out the door. They promise the church ladies they'll clean up and not leave the mess for me as they usher them out of the kitchen and through the front door. Finally, there is no one here except for family and Julie and Earl.

Earl and Daniel are in the back yard, where they've been most of the day. Junie and Daddy are in the living room talking, and Dianna joins them there as Julie and I put away the last of the dishes.

"We have a lot to talk about," Julie says. "I mean, look at you!"

"I'm sorry I couldn't tell you. I was afraid you would tell Earl."

"I would definitely have told Earl," she agrees.

"And he would have told Daniel as soon as he knew."

"I'm sure." She smiles sadly. "I'm glad your mom knew."

"Me too." I can't stifle a yawn.

"You need to rest, Liv. We'll talk later." She hugs me tightly. "You know I've got questions. Who was that guy?"

In spite of my grief and exhaustion, or maybe because of it, I giggle.

"I promise we'll talk soon."

She goes to the door and calls to Earl. Daniel stays outside while I walk them to their car.

"Thank you for keeping Daniel occupied," I tell Earl as we hug good-bye.

"Take care of yourself, Liv. Him, too. He's pretty broken up about your mom and everything."

Daddy is headed for the stairs when I come back inside. He kisses my forehead.

"Get some rest, sweetheart," he says. "It's been a hard day."

"Good night, Daddy."

It has been a hard day, and I don't know if the days will get better any time soon. The house already seems empty without Mama, even with all of us here. How will it feel when everyone goes back to their own lives and Daddy is left here alone?

I walk to the back door, expecting to find Daniel, but instead I find Aunt Junie and Dianna on the back porch, drinking wine and listening to the night creatures.

I go back through the kitchen and into the hallway.
"Daniel?"

"In here," he calls from the darkened living room.

"What the hell was he was doing here?" he asks as I flip on a lamp. I don't have to ask who he means.

"You heard him. He was worried about me."

"He has no right to be worried about you."

"He's a friend. Of course he has a right to be worried about me."

"You haven't known him long enough to warrant the kind of worry that makes a man travel hundreds of miles to check on you."

"I really can't have this argument tonight," I say wearily. "I didn't ask him to come. I didn't know he was coming."

Daniel sighs and pats the seat beside him. I drop

down on the sofa without a second thought.

"Come here. You've been on your feet too much today."

"What was I supposed to do, Daniel? Ignore the fact that he was here?"

"I don't know, Liv. All I know is that I didn't like him being here. I didn't like the way he hugged you. I didn't like the way he looked at you. You may not realize it, but that man feels much more for you than friendship."

I'm not about to tell him I know that, and that, for a while now, I've thought I just might feel more for him, too.

"I'm sorry," I say, because I am. "I really didn't know he was coming. I haven't talked to him since I came home."

The truth is I'm not sure how I feel about Peter coming to my mother's funeral. Was it a sweet gesture I should appreciate or an intrusion into a part of my life I'm not ready to share with him?

Daniel lays his hand on my belly. I place my hand over his, and for the first time, he feels the movements of our unborn daughter.

He jerks his hand away as if scalded and surges to his feet.

"Get some rest, Liv. I'll come by tomorrow to check on you and Oliver. Let me know if you need me before then."

He leaves me sitting there in stunned silence, the accusations he slung at the hospital coming back to me full force. It isn't until I hear the front door close that I leap to my feet and rush after him. I open the door just in time to see his car disappear down the road.

"Olivia," Junie says from behind me, and I realize

I've been standing in the open doorway for several minutes. "You need to get on up to bed and let that man sort himself out on his own. Nothing good has ever come from a woman chasing a man down and insisting he feel the way she thinks he should about things."

With a murmur of agreement, I shut the door and start toward the stairs. She puts a hand on my arm.

"The good ones figure it on their own," she assures me. "It just sometimes takes them longer than it should."

"Good night, Aunt Junie." I kiss her on the cheek. Then I pluck Mama's church sweater off the coat rack by the door and go upstairs.

Once in my room, I bury my face in the sweater. I inhale the lingering smell of her perfume and whisper to the baby.

"Your grandma loved the smell of gardenias."

After that, I list off several more things Mama had liked. When I finally drift off to sleep, I dream she is here in my room, holding my precious baby boy in her arms.

****

I'm packing my suitcase two weeks later when Daddy comes to my door.

"Daniel's here to see you," he says. "Do you want me to send him up?"

"Yes, I guess so. I should probably tell him I'm leaving."

Daniel comes by every afternoon to check on Daddy, but I've managed to avoid him altogether. Daddy says he asks about me, wants to know if I'm okay, but he hasn't sought me out. Until now.

"You're going back?" he appears at my bedroom door.

"I have to."

"When are you coming home?" he asks, but I know his real question is whether I'm coming home at all.

"I don't know."

He curses softly as I close my suitcase. Before I can lift it, he stops me. Cupping my face in his hands, he lowers his mouth to mine. It's our first kiss since I left him, and I'm unprepared for the raw passion of it. So familiar, yet so new, as if it's been decades since I felt his touch. Longing blossoms inside me as he deepens the kiss, his hands raking through my hair. He steps away, his hands still cupping my face, and looks into my eyes.

"I love you. No matter what else changes, that never will."

Then he grabs my suitcase and walks out of the room.

Dazed, I follow him slowly down the stairs. My father is waiting by the door. He hugs me tightly.

"See you soon, sweetheart," he says. He tries to smile, but it is a poor attempt.

"Are you sure you'll be okay? You can come with me, you know. Or I could stay."

"No, you have things to take care of there, and I need to be here. I'll be fine."

"I'll be back in a couple weeks," I assure him.

"I'll check on him while you're gone, Liv," Daniel promises when we reach my car.

"Thank you," I say, and he shakes his head.

"Don't thank me. After all these years, he's nearly as much my dad as he is yours."

"See you in a few weeks." I chirp, before the tears get the best of me. I am so tired of crying, but I can't seem to control it anymore.

His arms snake around me, and he kisses me again,

this time a softer, no less passionate meeting of lips and tongues, and maybe, I think, just maybe, hearts.

Chapter Twenty-Five

I can taste Daniel's lips on mine the entire drive to Key West. Part of me wants to turn around and run back to him. The other part of me tells me to keep driving. He's the one who made this mess; he's the one who will have to fix it. Neither part of me is sure what that will require. I know him well enough to know how sorry he is. I know he's not seeing Melanie anymore. I know his seeing her to begin with was an anomaly, out of character, out of the ordinary, so *not* Daniel. Yet it happened, and I'm afraid there will always be that niggling fear that it will happen again. It's that fear I'm not sure I can live with.

I know I can forgive him. I probably already have, truth be told. But I can't get past the fear of living the rest of our lives with even a hint of distrust between us. We might not be completely broken, but we're no longer as flawless as we once were. There's a crack, a fault line, a soft spot I'm not sure will hold the weight of us anymore.

I turn on the radio to drown out my own thoughts, and to fight back the sound of my mother's exhortations to come home. Then, I flip off the radio, just so I can hear her voice in my head. How I wish I had done as she asked, or at least attempted to make peace with her earlier. I'm so glad I asked her to come for the sonogram. I only wish I had known that would be the last time I saw her. My eyes blur with tears and I pull into a service station in the middle of the turnpike. I have a good cry, go inside for a bathroom break, a bottle of water, and a chocolate bar. Once I've cleared my mind and my head, I pull back onto the road and head south.

I breathe a sigh of relief as I drive onto Key Largo. I have always loved this string of islands, spread like pearls between the Atlantic Ocean and the Gulf of Mexico. I love the way the blue-green water stretches out as far as the eye can see. I love the sand and the sun, the crabs and the birds, and even the iguanas that have become rampant refugees on the islands. I love the very nature of the place, the laidback love affair the inhabitants have with their islands. When I'm here, I never want to go home.

Maybe this is home. The thought trots across my mind as I pull into Junie's drive. The slight breeze from the ocean, the scent of the ocean and citrus blossoms, the sounds of birds and lizards scuttling through the flowerbed combine with the smells of hot asphalt and restaurant cooking, the sounds of the tour trains and music from the tourist district to make that place that is uniquely Key West.

There's a note on the counter telling me Opal is sick and Junie and Dianna have gone to visit her. I find the nursing home number in the phone book and call to check on her. Junie comes to the phone and assures me Opal is fine, just crotchety and demanding a bit more of their attention than usual. I promise I'll visit her soon and hang up the phone.

The sound of laughter outside brings me to the window. Through the sheer curtains, I see a small group of people passing by, a thin older woman with short dark hair leading them all. She reminds me so much of Melanie Evans, I push the curtains out of the way. I haven't seen Melanie since the day I walked in on her with my husband, and I'm not sure why part of me hopes it's her. What will I do if it is?

I imagine myself waddling down the drive to confront her. "Hi, remember me? You screwed my husband the same day I found out I was pregnant with his kid."

I think of Junie, young and scared, pointing a pistol at her husband and his lover.

Could I hate someone that much? I sigh and let the curtain fall back into place. I'm not going to shoot Melanie, or even confront her.

The truth is, I would fight until the death *for* my husband and our marriage. I'd stand shoulder to shoulder with him, battling until we had conquered or been consumed by every wolf at our door. But I'd never fight *over* him. He isn't an inanimate object unable to make his own decisions, a two-timing carcass to be won by one vulture or the other.

Suddenly, the thought of Daniel's kisses turns sour, and I scrub a hand across my trembling lips. Just that quickly, all certainty I'm going back to Daniel is gone, and I stalk to the phone on the counter.

"Olivia?" Peter says when he answers my call. "I hope this means you're back."

"I am."

"Fantastic. I can't wait to see you."

"Will you be at the gallery in the morning?"

"Yes. The furniture is due to arrive at eleven."

"Great, I'll meet you there."

"I'd rather see you tonight. Will you come to me or

shall I come to you?"

A mild rush of panic makes my heart beat a little faster, and my head begins to pound. I can't see him tonight. Sadness and anger and sheer exhaustion have taken their toll on me, and my mind seems to have gone blank.

"I'm sorry, I..." My voice trails off.

"Of course," he assures me. "I'm sure you're tired from your drive. You and the baby need to rest. I will see you in the morning. I can't wait to show you the paintings I acquired while you were gone."

He doesn't seem to suspect I'm having doubts about staying in the Keys. Which is just as well, since I'm also having doubts about going home.

I call Daddy next because I know he'll be worried about whether I've made it. I'm not really surprised when Daniel answers the phone, and although I don't want to talk to him, I'm glad he's there with my father.

"I'm here," I say.

"You should be here."

"Just tell him I made it, and I'll call him soon."

"Olivia, please come home. We'll work everything out when you get here."

"Everything like what, Daniel? Like whether I can ever trust you again? Or whether you can love a baby you think isn't yours?"

"I know she's mine, Liv," he admits quietly.

"Bravo, babe. I knew you'd eventually add it all up and reach that conclusion. You always were good at math."

I slam the phone down before he can say anything else or before I can apologize for my waspishness.

****

I walk to the gallery the next morning, still fuming about Daniel. How dare he try to smooth things over with me? How could he ever even think I'd try to pass another man's baby off as his? How could he think I'd come back to him after what he did? How could he kiss me while my mother's death was still so fresh? That was unfair, and he knew it. I've never had any resistance to his kisses. The minute his lips touched mine, I was always done for. Even now.

I don't stop to wonder if my expanding anger is a convenient barrier against the ever-present grief that wants to take me to my knees.

I take a deep, calming breath as I walk into the gallery, and I'm immediately struck once more by the pure perfection of the place.

Peter is there, standing in the light streaming through the windows. He is the embodiment of the cliché: tall, dark, and handsome. Had Opal ever seen a man like this in someone's palm? As he leans down to kiss my cheek, I'm engulfed in the exotic yet wholly masculine scent of his cologne, and I wonder wildly if she ever saw *him* in mine. Pregnancy has surely addled my brain.

"It's good to have you back, Olivia," he says. "I was afraid I wouldn't see you again."

"I considered not coming back," I admit.

"But you did come back. That is all I care about."

I stroke my belly, and his mouth curls into a smile. He covers my hand with his.

"Was your husband happy about the baby?"

"Of course," I lie, stepping away from him. Knowing he let his mother- and father-in-law believe for the slightest of moments that my baby was his, I suspect he might take perverse pleasure in knowing Daniel also thought she was.

"Of course." His smile tells me he recognizes my lie for what it is.

"He wants me to come home," I tell him, sounding defensive. Daniel *is* happy about the baby.

"Are you? Going back to him?"

"No," I say. "I don't think so."

He chooses to ignore my uncertainty as he waves toward the pictures waiting at the other end of the room.

"Come, then, let's get to work."

****

"I'm meeting the children and Paulina's parents at the beach at one tomorrow. Why don't you join us?"

I look up from my desk as Peter walks into the small room we designated as an office. I've been back in the Keys for two weeks, and although he and I have been working feverishly to get the gallery ready, I'm still not sure I've made up my mind to stay. His children occasionally pop into the gallery with their grandparents, and I've joined them all for lunch several times. But I was able to pretend it was just part of my position at the gallery. An afternoon at the beach seems far more personal.

"I'll pick you up at noon," he informs me, taking my silence for agreement. "Wear your bathing suit."

I don't correct him, because my pregnancy hormones surge forth with a craving to see his bare chest and torso. I'm certain he'll wear a speedo, and although I've always found men in speedos a bit funny, the thought of him, looking like a fit, bronzed Adonis, with nothing but the bare necessities hidden, is enough to change my mind.

Chapter Twenty-Six

Daniel

Watching Olivia leave again is the hardest thing I've ever done. The thought of her seeing Peter Salazar again infuriates me, but I let her go because I can't make her stay.

I check on Oliver every day, and he seems glad for the company, although he doesn't say much of anything while I'm there. There are times as we sit there in silence that I am tempted to call Olivia, to demand that she come home, if not to me, then to her father. Like me, he is trying to be understanding, but I can see the hurt on his face every time I show up at his door without her.

He goes to the cemetery every morning and sits beside Sylvia's grave. I don't know what he does there, whether he talks to her or just recalls memories of their life together, but it seems to ease his pain somewhat and gets him out of the house for a little while, so I don't argue with him about it.

Since the day of Sylvia's heart attack, I've dried out, gone back to work, and tried to concentrate on making a better life for Olivia to come home to, even though I don't know that she ever will.

I lie in our empty bed at night, remembering the familiar way she melted into me when I kissed her. I want her home, in our bed, in my arms. I'm biding my time, giving her space, but soon, I'll go for her myself. And God help Peter Salazar if he tries to stand in my way.

It's been about three weeks since Olivia left when I stop by Oliver's on my way home from work and find him in his garage, working on a small wooden cradle.

"How are you doing?" I pull two beers from the six-pack I've brought with me and stick the rest in the refrigerator in the corner. I pop them open and hand one to him.

"Good as can be expected, I guess." He sounds resigned as he takes a sip of beer. "Just working on Olivia's gift."

I run my hand across the smooth wood. It's a beautiful little cradle, with hearts and flowered scrollwork carved into the wood.

"She'll love it."

He points to the top shelf of the garage where all that's visible are two evenly spaced wooden rockers. "I started one for Danny, but I wasn't quite finished with it. I was almost afraid to start this one. I guess you could call it an act of faith. Lord knows, Sylvia and I prayed long and hard enough. Then, seeing that tiny little thing moving around on the sonogram, how can I help but believe she'll be all right?"

I'm reminded once again how long Olivia kept this secret from me, how much I've already missed of our daughter's life. It seems unreasonably cruel of her, knowing that the months he lived in her womb were all the life our son ever lived, all the time we ever had with him.

"Sylvia told her she should tell you about the baby when we went down there," Oliver says as if reading my mind. "But Olivia's as stubborn as her mother at times, and she wouldn't budge on this."

"Sylvia told her I should know?" It moved me to know Sylvia had interceded on my behalf.

He lifts his eyes from the cradle.

"Sylvia loved you, son. She may have had a different way of showing it, and she was furious and hurt by what you did, but she always knew you were the man for our girl. Even before I did. I remember the first time you came to supper, on Olivia's birthday, she told me we needed to start saving for a wedding." He shakes his head, with a sad chuckle. "She was something else, wasn't she?"

"The finest mother-in-law a man could have."

"I know it hurts that Olivia didn't call you about the sonogram, but I can't regret that she called us. Olivia had barely spoken to us since she went to Junie's, and when she did, she and Sylvia were at each other's throats. So when she called and asked us to come down, we jumped at the chance. It was a short visit, but it was worth it. I've never seen anything so amazing in my life. Plus, Sylvia and Olivia came to some sort of peace agreement while we were there. I don't know how it happened, but it was good to see them at peace with each other for a change."

I remember the change in Sylvia the morning she collapsed. She'd insisted Olivia was coming home. That's why she'd cleaned so fast and furiously. As if Olivia's return was imminent. The truth is, when Olivia left three weeks ago, I would also have guessed her return was imminent. But she's still not home.

"Have you heard from Liv lately?" I ask.

"No. She was calling every day, but it's been a few days since she called. I've talked to Junetta, so I'd know if anything was wrong. Seems like the gallery opening's close, and she's real busy. How 'bout you? Have you talked to her?"

I shake my head, remembering the way our last conversation turned out.

"I don't think she wants to hear from me."

"Why wouldn't she? You two seemed to be on better terms when she left."

"We had a fight the last time she called," I admit.

"About what?"

"When I found out she was pregnant, I accused her of cheating on me. I told her I thought it was someone else's." I don't know why I tell him this.

"Peter Salazar's?" he asks without looking up.

"Yep. How'd you know?"

"He's the only man besides you I've ever seen Livy look remotely interested in. If I didn't know the baby was yours, I'd guess it was his, too."

"But it's not. Livy would never cheat on me. I know that about her."

"That's an awful lot of trust to put in someone."

"Trust based on fact isn't that hard."

He grins at me. "So why the hell did you tell her different than that?"

I'm ashamed of my answer even before I give it.

"I think I wanted it to be true, so we could be even. I could forgive her, she could forgive me, and life could go back to the way it was."

He shakes his head and sets the wood shaver on the work bench.

"Son, your life is never going to be the same. Life changes naturally, but when it's an unnatural change, like the one you inflicted on your marriage, then it's harder to adjust to. You can't equalize it. If she were pregnant with another man's baby, that would be worse than just cheating, wouldn't it? There would be a constant reminder of what she did, and it would sort of mute your own transgression."

I admit he's right.

"The first thing you need to do is accept the hand you dealt yourself. There's no breaking even here. For either of you. But that doesn't mean it's all gone. You just have to ante up with what remains." He chuckles and takes up the shaver again. "There's some rambling advice from an old card shark."

****

I stop at the grocery store on my way home from Oliver's. A stray cat has taken up residence on our back porch, and since he's done me the service of leaving two dead mice at the back door, I figure some cat food is the least I can do to repay him. Plus, I've run out of two of the basic food groups, coffee and beer.

I'm opening my truck door when I hear a familiar voice behind me.

"You are such a moron," Julie snaps, coming to peer down at my purchases. Earl stands behind her, looking both sheepish and amused. She picks up a can of cat food, and then the bag. "Is this what you're eating now?"

"No."

She rakes her gaze up and down my body. "You look better than you did at Sylvia's funeral. Thank God."

"Good to see you, Julie. Earl." I start to push past her, but she grabs my cart.

"How is Olivia?"

"Fine, I guess."

"What do you mean, you guess?"

"I haven't talked to her."

"What do you mean you haven't talked to her?" Her voice rises, and several shoppers look our way.

"I'm giving her space."

"You're a moron," she repeats her initial accusation.

"So I gather."

"Why the hell aren't you down there getting her?" She turns to Earl. "Tell him to go get her."

"I—"

"Earl will go with you," she interrupts me. "He'll go help you get her and bring her back."

"You want us to kidnap her?"

"If you have to," she says, then shakes her head. "But you won't. She loves you. You know that. So just go convince her you love her, too."

"She knows I love her."

"Does she?" Her skepticism throws me, but she's quick to expound. "How does she know that? By the way you were making it with that skinny little homewrecker? By the way you've wallowed in your own misery instead of worrying about hers?"

"I've told her I'm sorry. I told her I want her to come home."

"Did you honestly think the baby wasn't yours?" she demands, and I realize she's talked to my wife. My surprise must show because she rolls her eyes at me. "It's only you she isn't talking to now, dumbass."

I want to ask her if Olivia's still planning to live there, if she's really opening that damn studio with that man, and if she's ever coming home. Instead, I remain silent, and she lets go of the shopping cart.

"Daniel, I know losing Danny broke something inside her. All that love she had for that baby had nowhere to go, and after a while, having another baby became a bit of an obsession for her. I know it wasn't easy on either of you. And maybe some of that led to your affair with Melanie. But now it's time for you to fix it. You go down there, and you make her see your love. Repair what you broke, or neither of you will ever be okay again."

She surprises me by throwing her arms around me and hugging me tightly.

"Bring her home," she commands quietly. "That man isn't the right one for her. You are."

Chapter Twenty-Seven

Olivia

The children are waiting impatiently near the road when we arrive at the beach. Marc dances from one foot to the other, barely able to control his excitement as his father parks the car. Peter's cell phone rings, and he motions for me to go ahead and get out.

"Olivia! Father!" Marc calls as soon as I open the car door. My heart catches in my throat as he darts across the street without looking either way. "Look what I found!"

He rushes forward, his hand outstretched as he shows me the starfish he holds on his palm. The creature is still alive, his arms wrapping restlessly around the side of the child's hand.

"I told him to put it back," Adele announces from across the street. "I told him it would die if he didn't."

"Shut up, Adele," Marc says. "I'll put it back before it dies. Look at it, it's moving."

"It's trying to get away," his sister grumbles. "Isn't it, Olivia?"

"I don't think it will hurt to hold it another minute, but then you should put it back in the water."

I place my hands on his shoulders and he tilts his face up to look at me. "Marc, you ran across the street without looking both ways. What if a car had been coming?"

He blushes. "I'm sorry. I was just so excited to show the sea star to you and Father."

"I know, and I'm glad you wanted me to see it. It's beautiful, but I want you to be more careful from now on. Okay?"

He nods, and we both stroke the starfish with our fingertips.

"What do you have there?" Peter comes around the car. He admires his son's creature for a moment, then bounds across the street to grab Adele up and swing her around. The two of them dart toward the ocean. Paulina's mother shades her eyes, watching Marc and me come toward her.

"Marc," she scolds. "You didn't even look to see if a car was coming! You could have been killed!"

He has the grace to blush again. "I know, Grandmother. Olivia has already told me. I'm sorry if I frightened you."

His grandmother frowns at him for only a moment more before her face breaks into a smile. "It's okay, darling. I know you've been waiting to show Olivia your treasure. Now that she's seen it, perhaps you should let it go. You don't want to kill it."

He nods and dashes to the water's edge.

"Come, sit down, Olivia." She pats the empty beach chair beside her.

I lower my ever-increasing bulk into the chair. I wonder if I'll be able to get up when it's time to leave.

"What do you think of my grandchildren?"

"I think they're wonderful. I know you must be very proud of them."

She nods. "Yes, I am. I'm so happy that Peter and

Paulina shared them so freely. I hope that will not change."

"Why would it change?" I ask. "Peter seems to like the arrangement you all have."

"What about you, dear? Will the upheaval of the children coming and going be something you can handle?"

"I beg your pardon?"

"You will have your child and Peter will have his children. The blending of a family is difficult. Will sending the children to visit us disrupt the process, do you think?"

"I think you've misunderstood," I assure her. "Peter and I won't be blending our families. We won't be living together."

She shakes her head sadly.

"I never understood Paulina and Peter's living arrangement. She was such a beautiful, smart girl. I couldn't see why she would live that way just to keep him. I can't believe he's found another woman willing to do the same."

"What do you mean?" I warn myself it's none of my business how Peter and his late wife lived, but curiosity gets the best of me.

"She looked the other way, darling. Always. She tried not to see the signs or hear the rumors. She pretended they were happy living the way they did, but she wasn't. I know she wasn't. Even the name of the studio says it. Coeur Brisé. Broken Heart."

"But she lived here because of the studio, didn't she?" I ask. "Peter said she loved it here."

"Oh, she did. She loved it, but she would have moved to Atlanta in a heartbeat if Peter had agreed. She missed the children horribly."

"The children didn't live here with her?"

"Heavens, no. She wanted them to have a better education than they would have gotten here. So Peter kept them and sent them to a private academy closer to home. And she lived here alone. At the end, she was miserable."

I can't understand why Paulina left her husband and children in Atlanta if it made her unhappy to be without them. It's obvious her mother blames Peter for the way they lived, but I'm sure her mother's version of the story is somewhat biased in her favor.

Before she can explain further, Peter comes toward us, water beading his expansive, sun-bronzed chest. As I suspected, he is an Adonis in a speedo.

"Swim with us." He holds his hand out to me.

"I don't think so." I chuckle nervously. Despite my objections the day we met, his mother-in-law obviously thinks Peter and I are romantically involved. I don't want to add to that misconception by frolicking in the ocean with him and his children.

"Come on," he says and loosens my grasp on the arms of the chair. With gentle insistence, he pulls me to my feet and toward the water.

"Yippee!" Adele cries as I reluctantly follow him. "Play mermaids with me, Olivia."

I laugh as I imagine trying to move as gracefully as a mermaid in the water.

"I don't think I can be a mermaid, sweetie. Mermaids are beautiful and graceful."

She frowns at me, but then her face brightens.

"After you have the baby, you can be a mermaid," she says. "Now, you're under a spell."

"A spell?"

"Yes, a spell. A wicked witch put you under a spell."

"Okay."

"And the only way you can get out of the spell is if a handsome prince loves you and kisses you and breaks the spell."

"So why did the witch put me under a spell?"

"Because you were beautiful, and she was worried you would steal her boyfriend."

"Oh, well then, I must not have been a very nice mermaid."

"Yes, you were. You were very nice and very good. But she didn't know that, because she's a wicked witch, and she was afraid the prince would like you more because you're nice and good."

"The prince is her boyfriend?"

"Yes!" The child sighs in exasperation. "Do you understand now?"

I nod solemnly.

"Okay, good. I'm the beautiful fairy godmother, and I'm going to help you find the handsome prince."

I follow her lead as we pretend to look for a prince who can break the spell.

"Close your eyes," she finally says. "Magic only works if your eyes are closed."

I do as I'm told, and kneel there with my eyes closed, while she moves closer, spouting words of magical gibberish.

As her words end with a flourish, I feel someone rise out of the ocean beside me. Before I can open my eyes, he has me in his arms. His lips meet mine in a kiss that is far too passionate for either playacting or the audience we have.

"Peter! Stop!" I cry, pushing him away.

"Prince Charming!" Adele shouts like a miniature movie director.

"Prince Charming? No!" I correct as he reaches for me again.

I make a lumbering dash for the shore, his laughter following me all the way.

****

"Have you told your husband you aren't coming home?" Peter asks as he drives me to Junie's.

"No." I'm still a little perturbed he would kiss me in front of his in-laws and children. I'm more than a little perturbed that, despite the passionate nature of the kiss, I felt absolutely nothing.

"Have either of you filed for divorce?"

"No."

"Do you intend to?"

I'm not ready for that. I can't forget what Daniel did, but I can't forget the way he loved me either, or the way I love him.

"Paulina and I lived in separate cities most of our married life. It was a beautiful solution for both of us. Have you thought of that?"

"You loved her so much," I observe, although I am beginning to doubt whether he loved her enough. "How did the two of you bear living apart?"

He shrugs. "I loved her. That much is easy to explain. There was no stopping it. But things happen, people change. No matter how much you love someone, you can't always make them happy. She wasn't happy in Atlanta. I wasn't happy here. It made more sense for us to be in separate places. We could keep loving each other that way."

He chuckles at my obvious confusion.

"After a few years, Paulina and I were miserable together. We never could have stood each other twenty-four hours a day, seven days a week, fifty-two weeks a year. We would have murdered each other, I'm certain. At the very least, we would have ended up hating each other. I loved her too much to let that happen. Of course, there were others while we were apart. A man can't live for weeks on end without a woman to share his bed. You must accept it and put it out of your mind. Don't allow yourself to think about it. Paulina was a beautiful woman. I'm certain there were men here who enjoyed her beauty. I'm sure there were men here she shared things with that I will never know about. It doesn't bother me because I don't let it. Trust was never an issue between us."

"So you think I'm wrong to be upset with Daniel?"

"No, I'm saying you gave yourself no choice but to be upset with him. You gave him the power to hurt you and he abused that power. If you'd *never* trusted him so completely, then he couldn't have destroyed that trust."

"That is a horrid philosophy. So you cheated on Paulina?" I see clearly now that my notion of him as a loving, true-even-after-death husband is all wrong. I have the sinking suspicion that he isn't even someone I want to know, much less have any sort of relationship with, business or otherwise.

"No, but I slept with other women while we were married, if that's what you're asking."

"That's cheating!"

"Cheating hints at inflicting pain on your spouse. I never lied to Paulina, never hid things. What I did never hurt Paulina, and what she did never hurt me."

I have nothing to say to that, so I stare out the window, ready to leap from the car the moment we get to Aunt Junie's. Before he stops, he reaches for my hand, keeping me from fleeing.

"I want to open the gallery two weeks from Saturday. We have the artwork, and the studio is ready. There is nothing else to do. I've purchased the perfect dress for you. It will be here on Tuesday." I must look shocked by his audacity because he laughs and strokes my arm. "Paulina always let me dress her. I didn't think you would mind. You've had so much going on."

His hand moves up my arm, and he cups my neck, his thumb stroking my face. He leans close, his lips inches from mine.

"Promise me you'll be there with me, Olivia."

I know this is my halfway point, and I don't want to make a mistake I can't recall. He is a handsome man, and desire burns in his eyes. I lean toward him, my own desire fueled by the memory of his kiss in the studio weeks ago. I long to know if here, without an audience made of his children and in-laws, that passion will consume me once more.

There is no timid teasing as our mouths meet. It is a kiss of hunger and fiery desire. His touch leaves no doubt what he wants, as he seeks to claim me as his own. And I feel nothing at all. No passion, no desire. Nothing. I return his kiss, thinking perhaps it will stoke the flames. After all, I have dreamed of this since our last kiss. He doesn't seem to notice anything amiss as he deepens the kiss, presses closer in on me. A low moan escapes him as he cups my breast.

"I'm sorry, Peter," I say as I pull away from him and open my door. "I wish you the best, but I won't be at the gallery opening."

He is still sitting there when I close Aunt Junie's front door behind me. I stand there, with my back pressed to the door and my head whirling.

I want to think the things he and his mother-in-law told me today have killed my desire for him. That he could so casually discuss having extramarital affairs and pretend they didn't bother his wife, when her mother so clearly thought they did, is surely a good reason not to feel the kind of desire for him I thought I did. But I know better.

The truth is that what happened between our first kiss and our last has nothing to do with him and Paulina, but everything to do with Daniel and me.

What happened between then and now was the feel of my husband's kiss marking me as his own once again.

Chapter Twenty-Eight

It's hard for me to think of leaving Aunt Junie and Dianna, but I can hardly wait to get home. Last night in Peter's car was the turning point for me. I won't find my future in Peter Salazar's arms or his art gallery. My future is with Daniel Carson, just as it has always been.

I spent the night saying good-bye to the dreams I built in the months I was here, putting my relationship with Aunt Junie back in order, and preparing myself to return to a world that no longer includes my mother.

"Let us know when the baby's born, and we'll come right up," Aunt Junie says. "I may not be a mother, but I think I'm one hell of an aunt."

I laugh and hug her. "You would have done fine as a mother, Aunt Junie. But I'm really glad you weren't mine.."

Tears glimmer in her eyes as she touches my hair. "You wouldn't have turned out nearly as well if I were. That, I'm certain of."

Dianna comes out, holding a tiny box. "This belonged to my mother, and it came to me when she passed away. I always planned to pass it down to my own daughter, but I was never so blessed. You're the closest thing any of us broken old souls ever had to a daughter, and I want you to have it."

Inside the box is a beautiful necklace with a pink cameo of a mother and child.

"Dianna, are you sure? Maybe your son or one of his children would like it."

She looks at me sadly and shakes her head.

"I want you to have it, Olivia. Give it to your own daughter one day and share a kind word about the old lady who gave it to you."

We're all crying in earnest as she slips the chain around my neck, and I hug them good-bye one more time.

I'm backing my car out of the drive when Daniel's truck pulls up behind me.

Before I can even get out, he's there beside me, helping me to my feet.

"What in the world—" He silences me with a kiss. For once, I hold myself together, probing the kiss for the answers I need.

"I love you," he murmurs against my lips. "I love you."

He cups my face in his hands, and stares into my eyes.

"Liv, I'm sorry. Sorry I did what I did, sorry I hurt you, sorry I risked our life together. I know I can never make it up to you, but I will spend the rest of my life trying. Please give me that chance." He takes a shaky breath, brushes a tear from my cheek, and continues. "I know you can live without me, and since I'm still breathing, I can apparently live without you. But I don't want to. I want you. Permanently. Completely. Only you. I don't care where I live life, so long as it's with you. If you want Key West and you'll have me, then that's where I'll be, too."

I laugh through the tears streaming down my face.

"I was just on my way home, to you."

"You were?" he asks in disbelief. "Really?"

He kisses me again. This time, I give in to it completely, melting into him like I always have.

"Thank God!" Junie cries from the porch, and I realize she and Dianna are still standing where I left them.

****

That first night at home, I'm so exhausted I fall asleep the moment my head hits the pillow. I feel Daniel crawl into bed beside me, and I curl into him, lacing my feet with his, a habit I obviously haven't broken.

I wake up before he does the next morning, and I stay there, watching him sleep. He is so wonderfully familiar, yet it's like I've never seen him before. The horrible beard he had at the hospital is gone, and I can once again see his strong jaw and chin. In sleep, he is completely unchanged by the last few months, his brow smoothed and unlined. I reach out to run a finger over his lips, surprised by the tears that spring to my eyes. The sameness of him is heartbreaking when I know how much has changed.

His eyes open, and he looks at me. With a mumbled curse, he wraps me in his arms.

"Please don't cry," he murmurs against my hair, sounding as if his own heart is breaking.

The alarm goes off, signaling that it's time for him to get ready for work. I watch him get dressed, then follow him downstairs. As I put the coffee on, he takes a bag from the pantry.

"By the way," he says, heading for the patio, "we have a cat."

Through the glass door, I see him pour food into a bowl. A big, fluffy orange cat saunters up to the bowl, and Daniel runs a hand down its back while it eats. I shake my head in disbelief.

"I thought you hated cats," I observe when he comes back in.

"You can't really hate that one. He doesn't do anything but eat and sleep and bring dead critters to the door."

"What do you think other cats do?"

"I have no idea, but they aren't like George."

"George?"

"Yeah." He slips an arm around my waist and pulls me against him. "If Dooley comes over, don't let him outside. George kills rats bigger than him."

I laugh, and he kisses me softly on the lips before leaving.

Once he's gone, I go to the door nearest our bedroom and push it open. Once, this room was blue and contained a crib and all the other nursery furniture we thought we might need. After we lost Danny, we took the baby things away and Daniel painted the walls a light brown color he called marsh grass, which I despise. Once in a while, we store something in it, but it rarely stays longer than a week or two. For some reason, it seems this room will not lend itself to storage or anything else. Perhaps, I think now, it has always known it's a nursery.

As if to cement the fact that the baby and I are home to stay, I decide to get it ready for her arrival.

I start by buying paint at the local hardware store. I choose a peach-toned pink that reminds me of sunrise. I get a sample of it to take with me to the baby store, where I find a crib, a changing table, and lacy white bedding dotted with dainty embroidered flowers the same color as the paint.

While I'm there, I fill a basket with other things I know we'll need, including tiny gowns and matching caps and booties.

I can't help but smile as I slide into the car and feel the baby move. Every movement she makes brings us one step closer to her safe delivery. My obstetrician in the Keys assured me she sees no reason to worry and referred me to a colleague here who will take over my care. I have an appointment with her on Monday.

I push open the door to the house, my arms full of bags, and stop as soon as I'm inside. Daniel stands in the hallway, dressed in nothing but his dress pants, socks and a tie. The bags drop to the ground around me as I walk toward him. It's extremely hard to feel sexy with my belly the size of a large beach ball, but I attempt to sashay toward him anyway.

When I'm there, he pulls me to him, and our lips meet in a frenzied passion. We are both undressed in a matter of minutes. I'm not even sure how we make it to the bed, but he gently guides me down to it. I go willingly, completely absorbed in desire. I lie back while he rains kisses on my face, my neck, my arms. It is when he reaches my breasts that I am suddenly met with a memory of his eyes meeting mine over Melanie's shoulder. I try to force the memory away, but I am suddenly consumed by silent tears of heartbreak.

"Let me up," I moan. "Please Daniel, let me up."

He rolls off me immediately.

"What is it? Is it the baby?" he asks, concern evident in his voice.

I shake my head and dash to the bathroom before he can see my tears. He follows me, turning me toward him. He curses softly as he takes me in his arms.

"I'm sorry," he says, his own voice thick with tears. "I don't know what to do to make it better."

"I don't either," I sob against his chest, and I feel his own tears in my hair.

Chapter Twenty-Nine

When I wake up the next morning, I'm tired and achy. My back hurts and my feet are swollen. My puffy face is evidence of my intermittent crying jags during the night. Each time the tears started, Daniel would roll toward me, murmur soothing words, and take me in his arms. Yet I feel lighter, freer, as if a battle has been won. It's as if I cried myself out and am now ready to face the future unencumbered by hurt and regret. I know it isn't going to be as simple as it feels right now, with the early morning sunlight streaming through the windows. My mother is gone, my marriage is irreversibly changed, and life won't ever be what it was seven months ago when I burst through Daniel's office door. Still, I have hope that all will be well.

"What are you going to do today?" Daniel asks while he eats breakfast.

"I'm going to paint the baby's room."

"Liv, why don't you wait on that? I'll help you on Saturday. We have time, and I don't want you to overdo it. Plus, you have no business climbing up on the ladder to reach the tops of the walls."

"I bought an extension pole for the paint roller."

"Wait until Saturday," he repeats, more forcefully. "We'll get an early start, and have it done before nightfall."

"Fine," I grumble.

He chuckles.

"Don't spend all day pouting about it." He kisses me softly. "Get some rest. You didn't sleep very well last night. I love you."

I nod, and he turns to go.

I grab his arm before he can leave. "I love you, too. Be patient with me."

"Always," he says. "And forever."

I watch him leave and turn toward the nursery, intending to ignore his instructions. When I'm standing there, surveying the room, however, I change my mind. I really don't think I'm up to painting, so I go upstairs, hoping a shower will ease the ache in my back.

The shower doesn't help, so I try lying down, but that only makes it worse. Aggravated and irritable, I decide to go the cemetery to put flowers on Mama's grave.

Daddy is sitting on a bench under the oak tree, Dooley at his feet. Neither the dog nor my father is as spry as they once were, but both get to their feet when they hear my car door shut. They meet me halfway, and Daddy wraps me in a warm embrace.

"I'm so glad you're home, sweetheart."

'Me, too," I choke out, overcome by emotion.

He kisses the top of my head. "Come see your mother."

He takes my arm and leads me to the bench. It wasn't here the day we buried her, so I assume it's something he's put here since then. Dooley leaps up beside me, and I stroke his fur absently.

"I like to come by and just sit for a while. Sometimes, I bring the paper and a cup of coffee, sometimes, I just sit and think. I figured it couldn't hurt to have a place to sit. It's nice under this tree." He looks up at the branches of the tree. "When I was a boy, I sure would have loved to climb that thing."

I chuckle at that comment as we take a seat.

"How are things with you and Daniel?" he asks after a few minutes.

"They're okay," I say, but tears gather again, and I sigh in resignation. "I don't really know if they'll ever be okay again, Daddy."

"They will be. It just takes a little time and a whole lot of work."

"I thought it would be easier once I made up my mind to come back."

He shakes his head, a rueful smile on his face.

"Forgiveness isn't easy. If it was, it wouldn't be so precious to those who are forgiven."

"I think I've already forgiven him. I know he's sorry. But I can't seem to forget."

"No, I don't guess you ever forget something like that, but I think it gets easier with time."

"Mama said almost the exact same thing to me the night before you left Junie's."

"Your mother was an extraordinary woman, Olivia. I know she drove you crazy with her constant mothering. I know she could be overbearing at times, too, but she loved you as deeply as any mother ever loved her child."

"I know," I say. "I wasn't exactly kind to her the last few months."

"She understood. She knew you were hurt and angry. She understood, and she forgave you every angry word. You may not know this, but forgiveness was one of her greatest strengths."

I brace myself for the story Mama never told me but

I suspected. I'm finally ready to hear whatever it is that required her forgiveness. What he tells me is far different than what I'm expecting.

"Your mother never talked much about her family or her childhood, but it affected her entire life."

My mother never mentioned anyone in her family to me other than to say she had siblings and of course she had a mother and father, when I asked questions.

"She was the middle of five children. Her parents owned and worked a farm in Louisiana. From what I can tell, they were happy even though her parents struggled financially. Then it all fell apart. Her father had an affair. Her mother took all of the children and moved into an apartment in town. After a while, her father ended the affair. He begged her mother to come back to him. Your mama wasn't much more than a baby when it happened, and she loved her father to distraction. She joined him in begging her mother to go home. Her mother refused. She wouldn't budge, and her children suffered for it. She couldn't get anything but the most low-paying of jobs, and even those only lasted a few weeks at the longest. They were evicted time after time, food was scarce, and even the basic necessities were hard to come by. Sylvia's father tried to help them, brought money and food, tried to get them an apartment, but her mother refused his help every time. Swore she would never take a dime from him."

He takes a deep breath and runs a hand over Dooley's head.

"Eventually, when he threatened to take her to court, she took the youngest three children and ran. They ended up out west—Nevada, California, even Idaho for a while. But your grandmother never could make ends meet, and eventually, when your mama was twelve, she gave them all up to the State."

"She didn't send them back to their father?"

"No, she hated him so much she wouldn't even tell the State where they came from."

"What happened to them?"

"Your mama went to a foster family that treated her pretty well, although as soon as she turned eighteen, they put her on the street with nothing but a paper bag of clothes and a few dollars."

"What about the others?"

"She and I took a trip over to the little town where she grew up. Her dad had passed away, but she was able to connect with a cousin or two. She found out her oldest brother joined the army and died in combat and her oldest sister overdosed a few years later. She never was able to locate the two that went into foster care with her."

"How horrible!"

"Sylvia knew her father did wrong. But she felt like her mother could have forgiven him had she not been so hotheaded and full of hate. She said her father's actions may have broken their family, but her mother's actions shattered them all into a million pieces. She always believed if her mother had just tried to forgive him, they might have all survived."

"What happened to her mother?"

"She found her eventually, just before the old woman died. She was a nasty, bitter woman who told your mama in no uncertain terms what she could do with her forgiveness. I've never been prouder of my wife than when she leaned down over that bed, kissed her mother's wrinkled old head, and told her she was forgiving her anyway. When we walked out of that hospital, your mama's head was held higher than I'd ever seen it. It was like she'd exorcised a ghost from her soul."

He shook his head as if in wonder, a look of pride on his face.

It wasn't the story I expected, but it explained so much about my mother. The way she always insisted I at least try to control my emotions. The way she insisted I should try to forgive Daniel and make a life with him and our baby. How scared she must have been that her grandchild would end up like she and her siblings had, casualties of their parents' bad decisions.

"If I had known, I'd have been more understanding of her panic when I left," I tell him.

"You know she wasn't one to share those kinds of things."

"No."

"She was so frightened you'd make a rash decision and lock yourself into it. Like her mother. Like Junie. Especially after she met what she called your art gallery Lothario."

"Were you worried?"

"Not for a minute," he vows with a teasing grin. "I always knew my little girl wouldn't be led astray by a man she didn't love."

I put an arm around his shoulders and hug him to me. That's when I feel the first pain tighten my belly. I brush it off.

We sit in silence for a while, before Daddy stands to his feet.

"Time to go," he says, holding out his hand. "Let me treat you to lunch."

I don't feel like eating, but he looks so hopeful, I smile and nod.

"Sure, just give me a minute."

"I'll meet you at the car."

Kneeling in front of Mama's grave, I take one flower from the bouquet I brought with me and place it on Danny's tiny grave. I place the rest on hers.

"I love you," I say to them and try to stand.

Pain hits me when I'm halfway up, coming around my back and into my belly. I grab the cold granite of Mama's headstone and push myself to my feet, panting with the effort. I am barely upright when I feel a soft pop and a gush of warm liquid between my legs.

"Daddy!" I cry as I watch my amniotic fluid disappear into the cemetery ground. My eyes fly to Danny's grave, and I am overcome by terror.

Not again, I pray. Oh, God, please not again.

My father is there, helping me into his car. I dial Daniel's number, my hands shaking so badly I can barely push the buttons. A contraction overtakes me as I listen to it ring.

"Daniel," I cry when he picks up. "It's the baby."

Chapter Thirty

Daniel

I'm in the middle of a meeting with the development team for an open air mall my firm is designing when my cell phone begins to ring.

I excuse myself when I see it's Olivia.

I hear her panting before she speaks.

"Daniel," she gasps, her breathing labored. "It's the baby."

I know she doesn't realize this is almost exactly what she said the day our son died, but the familiar words hit me in a rush that nearly causes my heart to stop.

"My water broke," she says. "I'm having contractions. Daddy is driving me to the hospital."

"Your dad's there?" Thank God she isn't alone.

"Yes, at the cemetery. I came to put flowers on Mama's grave." Her voice rises in pain. "Oh, Daniel."

"Breathe, babe. Just breathe."

Earl steps out of the meeting. "Everything okay?"

"It's the baby."

"Go!" he commands. "I'll take care of things here. You go to Livy."

I'm already moving down the hall, into the elevator, the phone still pressed to my ear. I can hear Olivia praying on the other end of the line.

"Please don't take her. Not again. Please, Lord." Her

voice is so faint and breathy, I can barely hear it.

"Liv, the baby is not going to die. Do you hear me? You're both going to be fine. I'm getting in the car now. I'm on my way."

It's too early, I think, as I fumble with the key. She's not nearly as far along as she was with Danny. I remember her as she was just after his birth. She'll never survive it again.

I hit the accelerator, heedless of the speed limit. I can't let her face it alone again. I need to be there when they tell her the news.

I rush through the hospital doors.

"My wife's here," I tell the nurse at the desk. "Her name is Olivia Carson. She's in labor. Too early."

"Your wife arrived a little while ago." She points to the elevator across the lobby. "She's already been taken up to labor and delivery. Fourth floor. I'll let them know you're on your way up."

A middle-aged blonde in scrubs meets me at the elevator. "Mr. Carson?"

"Yes. Is my wife okay?"

"She's fine," she says. "Follow me."

I've walked this hall before, and I'm not reassured by her words. She leads me into a small room, where she hands me a set of green scrubs. I slide them over my clothes, and she hands me a mask, cap, and shoe covers. "These, too."

She directs me to a sink, and once she deems me sterile enough, she pushes open a door to the delivery room. Olivia lies in the bed, her legs in stirrups and her eyes closed.

"Thank God," Oliver says from the other side of her. His eyes above the mask are worried, but they crinkle a bit when he meets my gaze. "I'm going to make my exit now."

He clasps my arm and slaps my back as he passes.

"Some things are beyond a father's realm," he tells me.

"Is this your husband, Olivia?" the doctor asks, and Olivia turns toward me.

"Yes." She smiles sleepily.

I'm reassured by her smile, but I look to the doctor for confirmation.

"Your wife is in labor, Mr. Carson. We're going to deliver your daughter today." His calmness is contagious, and I relax a little as he looks back at Olivia. "Let's see what this next contraction brings, shall we?"

The nurse who brought me in waves me over to the bed. Olivia's eyes are closed again. The contrast between her near hysteria earlier and her current stillness is stark and concerning.

"Liv?" My voice is sharp with alarm.

"She's had a bit of medicine to help her relax, so she's a little groggy," the nurse assures me. "You're going to stand right here, and when the doctor says to push, you're going to support her back while she pushes."

As if on cue, the doctor instructs Olivia to begin pushing. The nurse puts my hand on Olivia's back, and together we bring her forward while she squeezes her eyes shut and pushes with all her might.

"Okay," the doctor says. "Rest for a minute, Olivia. The next couple pushes should do it."

The nurse steps out of my way, and I look down at Olivia's face. She's more beautiful than I have ever seen her.

"Here comes another one, Olivia," the doctor says. "One more big push."

As she pushes, I watch the doctor like a hawk, trying to gauge his reaction to what's happening. He smiles up at us.

"She's crowning," he tells us. I might look a bit confused, because he adds, "I can see the head."

Seconds later, Olivia is pushing again, and I watch in amazement as the baby slides into the doctor's hands.

Olivia goes limp, and I gently lower her back to the bed. Her eyes are wide with fear as she clings to my hand.

"Is she alive?" she whispers at the same moment the baby lets out a lusty wail.

"Mr. and Mrs. Carson, meet your new daughter," the doctor says as he places the tiny squalling infant on Olivia's chest.

Chapter Thirty-One

Olivia

Daniel looks down at me as the nurses take the baby from my chest to wash her up.

"She's fine," I say. "Perfectly fine."

"All six pounds four ounces of her," he beams.

"Thank you."

"You did all the work." He grins at me.

"You had a little something to do with it," I remind him. I run a hand over his chest. "You should wear scrubs all the time. You're the hottest doctor here."

He laughs and kisses my hand. "You're exhausted and drugged."

"But not blind."

The nurses bring her back, clean and swaddled. Her dark eyes shine up at me from beneath the little pink cap on her head. I can think of nothing to say as I stare into those eyes, already so much like her daddy's.

She opens her tiny rosebud mouth and turns her head toward my breast. I place her to it and watch, fascinated, as she sucks a few times, before she falls asleep.

I look up at Daniel. Tears course down his cheeks, and I reach up and brush them away.

"Don't cry," I say. "We're going to be all right."

With our child in my arms and my husband at my side, I can believe nothing less. I pray that one day the past few months will just be a footnote in the life we've created together.

I think of Mama and her broken childhood, telling me forgiveness is possible, and Daddy telling me what a gift it was to watch her forgive her mother.

I think of Corliss of the blue fingernails and lost baby. I think of Dianna of the abused body and stolen child. I think of Harry of the broken wife and undying devotion.

I think of Opal, her body being slowly eaten by illness and old age, folding my hand closed and making her prediction about my happy ending.

Finally, I think of Junetta Darlington, the aunt who gave birth to me and loved me enough to give me to the parents who adored me. I remember her assurance that love can't be killed by pain or mistakes, and I know now she's right.

****

Two days later, Daniel and I bring Ava Rose Carson home. A bundle of pink balloons is tied to the porch railing, and I look at him questioningly.

"Your dad, Junie, and Dianna were here earlier. They made you some lunch and helped me finish up in the nursery. They thought you'd need to rest when we got home, so they're at your dad's. But they'll be back later."

He carries the baby into the room which has been miraculously transformed into a beautiful nursery since I left three days ago. As I survey the room, my eyes fall on the small wooden cradle in the corner.

Inside it is a pink patchwork quilt. Tears spring to my eyes when I recognize Mama's handwriting on the envelope that rests on top. It contains a single sheet of matching stationary. I can almost hear her voice as I read it.

I certainly didn't need Opal Horowitz to tell me you were having a girl. I had already spoken to the good Lord about how much you needed this baby to be a girl after what happened with Danny. And for the record, I started this quilt before we ever saw the sonogram. Love, Mama.

I laugh as I fold the note and put it back in the envelope. Leave it to my mother to find a way to prove she's right, even from the afterlife.

****

Night is falling when I wake up from the nap Junie insisted I take while they were here to help with the baby.

The house is silent except for Daniel's low voice humming an old rock song. I follow the sound to the living room, where he's sitting on the sofa with his feet propped up and Ava cradled in his arms. She looks so small but so perfect.

"Are they gone?" I ask quietly.

"Yes. How was your nap?"

"Awesome."

The baby turns her head to root against his arm.

"You're just in time." He grins as I come toward them.

I slip into the space between his body and the arm of the couch, and he gently passes her to me. He watches her nurse, his arm around my shoulders. His hand strokes my hair.

I lean against him, savoring the feel of the three of us here together. In the silence, I remember Junie's words to me the day she told me about Corliss.

In reality, we were a group of broken people who

came here to find solace and stayed here because together we were closer to whole.

I look up at my husband. A broken man, loving a broken woman, both of us fighting for a family broken nearly beyond repair. A sense of peace falls over me, and I suddenly understand what she meant. Together we are closer to whole.

Chapter Thirty-Two

Standing on Aunt Junie's veranda, I watch the street below. Daniel is coming up the sidewalk, our three-year-old daughter, Clara, on his shoulders. I wonder if he even knows chocolate ice cream is dripping from the cone in her hand, down her arm and into his dark hair. Ava trots along beside them, licking a cone full of strawberry ice cream and keeping up a steady stream of conversation.

Junie comes to stand beside me, wrapping an arm around me, and I lean my head on her shoulder.

"I'm glad you came," she says.

"I wouldn't have missed it for the world. Opal always did know how to put on a show."

She chuckled. "We should have known she'd want to do a reading from the great beyond."

"Who knew she would talk the minister into not giving us all a warning before the lights were lowered and her voice came bellowing out of the speakers."

"Can you imagine what your mother would say?"

"Absolutely." I laugh at the thought. "I can hear every word."

Daniel whistles at us, and we look toward him. He and the girls raise their hands, and I blow them a kiss, while Junie waves.

"What are the two of you doing out here?" Dianna asks, coming to stand beside us.

"Thinking Opal was right."

She places a hand on my rounded stomach. "Another girl?"

"Probably." I agree. "But I was thinking about the day we went to visit her in the nursing home. The day she told me Ava was a girl."

"She read your palm, didn't she?" Dianna says.

I nod and open my mouth to remind them what she said.

"Mama!" Ava calls from downstairs. "C'mon! Daddy says we can get in the pool!"

Junie chuckles and places a kiss on my cheek.

"Go on," she whispers. "Your happy ending is calling."

A word about the author...

Gloria Davidson Marlow's heart is firmly planted in northeast Florida, where she grew up in a family of commercial fishermen, married her high school sweetheart, and raised their children. A paralegal at a local law firm, she loves baking, canning, thrifting, and spending as much time as possible with her husband, children, and grandchildren.

Thank you for purchasing
this publication of The Wild Rose Press, Inc.

For questions or more information
contact us at
info@thewildrosepress.com.

The Wild Rose Press, Inc.

CPSIA information can be obtained
at www.ICGtesting.com
Printed in the USA
LVHW012207031022
729859LV00014B/474

9 781509 244539